Embers: Beastly Curses

by Sky Sommers

Table of Contents

Sky's books in the Magic Kingdoms series:
Cinders: Necessary Evil
Embers: Beastly Curses
Ash: Crooked Fates

Short stories related to the Magic Kingdom:
To Cure a Curse (a Belle & Beast novella)
To Make a Wish (before and after for Grizelda the Witch)
To Thaw a Heart (a Snow Queen novella)
Three Rocking Pigs (the full Three Little Pigs retelling Marina read to Henry)

Goddesses Series:
Charm & Mayhem: The Goddess of Fate (begins when Grizelda/Marina gets back to Earth)
Life & Death: The Goddess of Light (about Ellie & Victor from Ash)
Love & Money: The Goddess of Luck (about Hans wooing Dita)
Fire & Ice: The Goddess of Frost (about Ava and Zack from Goddesses: The Bet)

Standalone prequel to Goddesses Series:
Goddesses: The Bet

Standalone novels related both to Magic Kingdom and the Goddesses of Fate:
Thumbelina: The Bride Experiment (about Loretta the pixie)
King of Time (a Magic Kingdom prequel featuring Fate that explains the fountain in Cinders)
Someone To Watch Over Me

Also, look out for Tales From the Magic Kingdom (short story sets):
Tales of the Mirrors
Tales of the Shoes
Tales of the Dragons

Short stories in multi-author anthologies:
To Kiss a Frog – Marina disenchants her baby daddy in Enchanted Waters
To Snare a Prince – Greta meets Eddie in Enchanted Forests
To Steal a Kiss – Greta uncurses Eddie in Enchanted Flames
To Find a Queen – Nefarious' POV of Greta meeting Eddie in Twice Upon a Name
Yumiko's Revenge – magic shoes aid vengeance in Once Upon a Name
The Dance of Death – Death & Fate work together to help a starving artist in Slightly Sweetly, Slightly Creepy
To Spot a Swan in Third Name's a Charm

Dystopian:
This Time Around

For my Grace and all the Graces out there
who think the mirrors are lying to them and
who would give anything to keep their family together.

Prologue

A man sporting a few rabbit and fox pelts on his belt knelt by the sheep whose throat had been ripped out. Another animal lay in a pool of blood a few feet away.

'So, Peter, do you reckon it's…?' The farmer asked, leaning on the fence, with a pitchfork in hand.

Peter rubbed his stubbled jaw and gave a curt nod. 'Seems so.' He hoped against hope it was not his wolf. Maybe she got fed up with the toads and the mice aplenty in the underbrush. Maybe she just wanted a decent meal. He ruffled his chestnut hair. Still, once a predator had had a taste for sheep, it would keep coming back for more of that easy prey. He would have no problem tracking down and making sure the rogue was eliminated. Provided it wasn't her.

Anyone but her.

'So, I was right. This was a wolf's doing.' The farmer gripped the handle of his weapon tighter. 'Now you see why the huntsman's post is open in our tiny nook of the Magic Kingdom. You'd be well suited for the job, Peter.' The farmer motioned at the pelts. 'Interested?'

Grey eyes flashed in the bright morning light as Peter stood up to his full height, towering over the farmer who trusted him enough to ask for his opinion. 'I know the village is going to be adiddle with getting revenge. Before you lot storm into the woods with pitchforks and torches and do yourselves more harm than anyone else, let me investigate.'

The man scratched his neck. 'Well… if you tell the village elder you accept the post and sniff out where the pack lives, I guess you'd be better suited to mete out justice.' He ogled the rifle hanging off Peter's shoulder.

1. The Black Wolf

Peter

The huntsman stopped to listen. The forest swished and murmured around him.

A wolf howled.

The huntsman turned and stared into the darkness as if willing it to take shape.

Another wolf joined the lament.

Then another.

And another.

Peter's heart sunk somewhere below his ribcage.

Wolfsong.

A wolf was dead.

The pack was mourning.

Peter knew he had mere days to find the corpse and put it to good use. Get the pelt. If the corpse was too mangled or rotten, set it up as if it had fallen into one of his traps. Anything to make it look like it was him who had killed the wolf. To appease the villagers. To keep his job.

He hoped it wasn't the black female. She was smart. She wouldn't get caught in traps and as the pack's dedicated nanny she was used to dismantling fights, not getting into them.

Over the past year he had learnt to differentiate her throaty howls from the others'. He had learnt that every wolf had its own pitch. Not that she howled a lot. That would be out of character for her. It was too emotional a way to communicate.

Peter remembered the first time he had spotted the black mas- tiff-sized female wolf standing at the edge of the forest, looking right at him. He, the twins and three-year old Henry had just moved here, and there she was. A wolf staring at him from the underbrush.

His heart had leapt into his throat.

At least she was going to be easy to spot. Or so he thought.

She had proved him wrong on many counts. The black wolf went into hiding, joined a pack and he had rarely seen her since that first encounter. If he hadn't been on the look-out for her black fur, he wouldn't have noticed her trailing him and Henry in the woods.

The last eerie notes dissipated above the darkened tree-tops. The huntsman adjusted his rifle and started toward the sound. He wasn't going to sleep a wink anyway. Not until he found out if she was alive.

Summer

'I know it's you, so just come on out,' Peter said, tucking an errant strand of his brown hair behind his ear to see more clearly.

A black wolf stepped out from behind the pine tree.

'There you are.' The huntsman crouched down. 'I'm not going to hurt you. You've helped me find your dead kinsmen even though you know what I do with them afterward. I would never hurt someone who helps me.'

The wolf barked with her head down.

'Are you laughing at me?'

The wolf shook her head.

'Why don't you come closer?'

The wolf darted behind the tree again. Three small pups peered from the ferns at the base of the tree and sniffed the air. The she-wolf towered over them protectively and pawed at the pup who was trying to incite others to play.

The man stood up. 'Yours?'

The wolf shook her head again.

'Babysitting?'

The wolf nodded.

'You don't want my smell on them,' the huntsman said and the wolf nodded again.

'Are you teaching them to hunt?'

Another nod.

'Don't teach them to hunt humans,' the huntsman said sternly.

The wolf gave another curt nod.

A shaky truce then.

The huntsman stared at the black beast's unnaturally green irises and ran his fingers over the grass, wishing he was stroking that black fur instead.

They stared at each other until one of the pups whined. The she- wolf nudged the trio back into the underbrush and with one last look at the huntsman disappeared after them.

Autumn

The black wolf stood at the edge of the forest and watched the young man with a mop of flames for hair work his magic. He had grown in the last two years and looked older than he was.

Swish, thwack! Swish, thwack!

The firewood fell into two neat piles next to the old tree stump the youngster was using as a chopping block. There wasn't a wayward splinter in sight.

The wolf's ears flickered as she stared at the huntsman's abode.

Swish, thwack! Swish, thwack!

'Hans, don't you think you've chopped enough?' Peter appeared in the doorway, wearing leather getup.

'Nope.'

Swish, thwack!

The wolf lay down and kept her eyes on the house with the thatched roof, the three steep steps of which were adorned with pumpkins of various sizes. It looked like a parade of decapitated heads more suitable for Scarecrows than human lodgings. Candles tucked into the vegetables illuminated their triangled eyes and uneven horrible teeth from within the vegetable. A few fox skins and some delicious rabbits were hanging from the rafters, but while those made her mouth water, they were not important.

Where was the boy?

The wolf saw a girl of fifteen peek out of the logged house, with a small raven-haired boy of about five clutching her hand.

She kept her eyes on the boy and took a step forward. All her instincts told her to howl with frustration because she wasn't able to get to what was hers. The wolf swallowed the sound and coughed instead.

The girl turned to the forest. 'Who's there?'

The wolf stilled as the huntsman ordered. 'Greta, Henry, come on in. Hans, you, too. That's enough for today.'

Without a word, Hans carefully cleaned his axe with a linen cloth from his pocket. Satisfied, he stomped inside.

The wolf kept her gaze trained on her target.

The little boy reappeared, turned to the forest and looked straight at where the wolf was hiding. 'I know you're there,' he whispered and the wind carried his words to the wolf's perked-up ears. Her snout formed something akin to a smile.

Winter

Peter crouched down in the snow.

Paw marks.

The front one had elegant elongated toes.

It was her.

He still couldn't bring himself to say her name out loud.

Grace.

He had seen her turn.

Two years ago, on their rooftop.

He knew who she was.

Who she had been.

Who she would never be again.

Peter looked at the boy gathering firewood mere feet away.

He didn't blame him, albeit Henry was the reason for his and Grace's relocation to the Magic Kingdom from swanky London, Earth dimension. Peter couldn't blame his son. He knew Grace would do the same over again, darn the consequences and so would he. To keep the family together. Almost losing a mother at birth was hard enough. Losing her again at age three had been devastating. The boy, who hadn't been talkative to begin with, had shut down. They hadn't heard a peep from him the entire summer following Grace's disappearance. 'Henry, don't go too far, okay? Don't stray from the path. Never stray from the path.'

The boy nodded and reached for another fallen branch.

Paths in this forest were tricky even without the wolves.

Peter watched the boy, hoping that the animal hadn't taken the black wolf over completely. That she would remember enough of her previous life to not eat her own son.

Another six months later...

2. The Witch

At the hut

The witch put a cauldron on the fire. She was expecting company and she was hungry.

It had been a long while since Hans and Greta's visit.

The boy should be here soon, if the mirror was anything to go by.

With pancakes and strawberry jam, right out of one of Grace's fairytales.

The witch chuckled and licked her lips as she looked at the giant bronze mirror that showed Time had been kind to her. She didn't have many crow's feet. Nor had she gained weight and even though her hair was grey and wispy, it cascaded down her back in lush waves.

She turned away from her mirror, remembered Hans and Greta fondly and thought how hungry she was. She'd have something tastier than pancakes in no time.

If only the boy would hurry up and get here.

3. A Walk in the Woods

Henry

Halfway to Granny's the five-year-old raven-haired boy in a red T-shirt stopped to hook his other hand through the basket handle. That's when he heard the rustle.

'Who's there?'

Silence.

'Are you hiding?' the little boy asked the two green eyes that had lit up in the ferns, five feet away at the base of a pine tree.

He got a blink in return and a black snout appeared.

'It's you!' The boy exclaimed. 'I've seen you before. I'm... I'm Henry. Not that names matter to you. Do wolves have names?'

The she-wolf nodded.

'What should I call you?' Henry asked. 'Wolfie?'

The animal coughed and it sounded like a raspy laugh.

'Are you afraid of me?'

This time, he got a head-shake.

'Are you the big bad wolf the whole village is talking about?'

The animal gave a few slow nods.

'You ARE big. Are you bad?'

The wolf shook her head again.

'Then why do they say you are?'

The wolf chuckled again.

'Yeah, Wolfie, you can't talk. I get it. I didn't talk for a whole summer once. I didn't want to. I had to say something when the village kids started taunting me by calling me 'Red, Red'. I think it's because of my shirts. Now everybody calls me Red. Even Granny. She says it with affection though. Then I don't mind.

Much. Although why they don't call Hans that, I have no idea. He's the one with red hair.'

The eyes disappeared and reappeared only two trees away.

'Hey, you crept closer.'

A nod.

'Do you plan to eat me, Wolfie?'

Another head-shake.

'Would you tell me, if you did?'

The wolf nodded.

Henry shrugged. 'Well, I guess it's okay then. As long as you don't lie.'

The black wolf shook her head, perked up her ears, sniffed the air once and kept advancing, her eyes fixated on the boy.

'What'cha doing?'

The wolf seized the boy by the tail of his shirt and pulled him into the thicket.

'Hey! You said you weren't gonna eat me!' Henry swatted at the wolf. 'I hope you didn't ruin my favorite shirt,' he mumbled, inspecting his red T for holes.

A carriage drawn by four horses bounded past.

'Oh.' The boy stared at the clouds of dust the vehicle left in its wake. 'Thank you. But don't do that again!' Henry waved his finger at the animal.

The wolf shook her head and put her snout in the boy's palm as they returned to the path.

Henry scratched his wolf behind her ears and kept ahold of her fur as they kept walking. From behind, it looked like a boy of five was walking his huge black mastiff in the woods.

'It's my favorite shirt, see.'

The wolf barked her coughing laugh.

'If I asked Greta for a hooded shirt, do you think they'd start calling me Little Red Hood?'

Wolfie laughed again.

The boy patted her head. 'You know, I think you can talk. In your own way.' He got a nod in return.

When they came to a hut towering on what seemed like two giant stilts, the wolf shook the boy's hand off her mane and disappeared into the woods.

An old woman in a poppy skirt appeared in the doorway and grabbed for the railing to steady herself as the hut decided to stretch its chicken legs.

'Grandma Grizelda!' The boy waved, standing a few feet away from the hut, watching the legs perform their gymnastics. 'I brought you pancakes!' He waved the basket at her.

'Enough!' She ordered and the hut stilled. 'The birds aren't singing. Henry, get inside,' the woman said tersely, eyeing the quiet woods. She whistled once. The hut quacked and sat down, folding its legs underneath.

Henry nodded and climbed the three dilapidated wooden steps.

The old woman closed the door after him and walked halfway to the woods, whistling once to make the hut rise up again.

'I know you're there. I've seen you,' she addressed the trees.

Her statements were met with eerie silence.

'I know how you hunt. In packs. No animal takes that long to stalk their prey and contrary to the imbecilic villagers, I know you don't eat humans.'

Two huge eyes appeared in the underbrush, mere feet from her.

'Your eyes are green,' the witch said and squatted. 'Now why is it that every wolf I've seen in my life has yellow eyes and you don't? Are you guarding him?' The witch asked.

A lone bark sounded.

The witch smiled.

'Saves me time walking him back in that case. My legs ain't what they used to be.' Grizelda sighed.

She took something from her apron pocket and laid it down in the ferns under the nearest tree.

'I'm guessing you're hungry from all the trekking. Here's some bread, if you like. I'll send him on his way tomorrow morning. He'll be staying the night.'

When she turned to look from her doorstep, the bread was gone. 'And when you're done escorting him home, come back, I want to have a proper chat with you. Tomorrow.'

4. The Proper Etiquette with Wolves

At the hut

'Red, I have to talk to you about wolves,' Granny said when she came back inside. A lone cauldron hung over the fire and a pitcher of water was set in the middle of a long wooden table. Apart from a white cloth hanging in the corner the room housed one armchair, a bench and the tiniest of kitchens with a miniature stove.

Two bright eyes looked back at her. 'I like wolves. They are nothing like in the story-books, you know.' Henry pointed at a picture in a book.

Granny took the book away from him. 'Yes, but do you know why people wrote down stories like that? Because sometimes, little children went missing in the woods and were never found later. It almost happened to your own brother and sister.'

The boy nodded. 'I know, Granny. But my wolf…'

'*Your* wolf?'

'Yes, my wolf. She's kind. She just saved me from being run over by a carriage. Why would she do that if she wanted to harm me?'

'So she could eat you herself?'

The boy pulled his mouth taut and shook his head vigorously. 'No. She protected me. She walked me here. And she can talk. Well, kind of. You talked to her yourself. I heard you.'

Granny sighed. 'I think your wolf might be magic. But not every wolf you meet is going to be. I have to teach you the proper etiquette with wolves.'

'Etiquette?' Henry asked.

'The way to act around wolves,' Granny explained. 'Next time you see a wolf that you don't know, just observe him or her at first. They are afraid of people. We are the only ones who can harm them. So, it's very rare for a human to see a wolf. If you do, either the wind is from them to you and they didn't smell you or

11

it's a young one and they are curious. They don't eat humans, at least not when the forests are full of deer and elk, and famine is as far from the village as the sea. Try not to stare lone wolves in the eyes,' Granny said. Seeing Henry's attention wavering, she held his chin up. 'Listen. If it's summer and you see a mother with cubs, she might be teaching them how to hunt. What's most important, if the wolf tries to come near you, see if it's healthy. If the fur is patchy, worn out or balding, then the wolf is ill and all you need to do is make a scary noise or throw something. That will spook them. They don't know how to throw and they are easily spooked by something new. Throwing would be new.'

'Okay but what about my wolf? How come she is comfortable around me?'

'Well, there could be two reasons. Either you're special or she is,' Granny said.

The boy's eyes goggled. 'I'm special?'

Granny ruffled his hair. 'We already know you're special.'

'But my wolf is also special.'

Granny though about it. 'She could be. Maybe she isn't afraid of you because she is used to being around humans from a young age. Maybe someone rescued her when she was a cub and she got used to humans? I don't know. I'd still be careful, if I were you.'

'But she wants to be my friend. I don't want to throw things and spook her off. I like her.'

Granny pursed her lips. 'Let me talk to her to see if she is magic and if she is good. Then you can be friends, okay?'

The boy thought about it for two seconds and then nodded. 'How come you know so much about wolves?'

Granny shrugged. 'Nature channel.'

When met with a bewildered stare, the old woman smiled. 'I meant I'm a keen observer of Mother Nature. Shall we eat then?'

Red nodded and carried the two plates and cutlery Granny got from her cupboard to the table.

'Wait, put them in that corner, we need to get the table cloth first,' Granny said.

'What's for dinner?' Henry asked, casting curious glances at the idle stove. He peeked into the cauldron and was disappointed to find only boiling water.

'What do you want for dinner, dear?'

'Pancakes,' Henry said and looked wistfully toward the basket he brought. 'Except that's dessert. Papa always says savory before sweets.'

'Yes, pancakes, in a minute. What savory things would you like?'

'Granny, I didn't bring anything like that and it looks like you didn't have time to make food, it's ok, I'm not hungry.'

The witch tousled his hair. 'Don't you worry about any of it. Tell me, are veal cutlets still your favorites?'

The boy nodded eagerly.

'Well, then. I think it's high time Granny showed you how she always has everyone's favorite dishes ready.' The woman winked.

She took a ratty linen table cloth and set it down on the table, then leaned in and whispered something to it.

The boy held his breath as dishes started appearing out of nowhere - a steaming pot of soup, a plate of mouthwatering cutlets, a bowl of mashed potatoes and a platter of vegetables.

He looked at Granny in wonder. 'Is that what I think it is?'

The witch nodded.

'How come you have the magic dinner cloth, the *skatert-samobranka*?'

'You have been paying attention to the old Russian folktales I've been reading you. Good boy.' The woman beamed. 'As for how I got it - it came with the hut. And everyone who knows the folk tales like we do,' the witch winked, 'already knows the magic words to say.'

The boy ran his fingers over the linen cloth that was no longer ratty, but starched and gleaming white.

'First time it has done that,' the old woman mused. 'She must like you a lot.'

'Thank you for our food,' Henry whispered to the cloth and a bowl of raspberries popped up next to him.

'I'll pack the leftovers so you can take them home with you tomorrow,' Granny said.

'Won't they disappear on the way?'

'Well, do you think the food in your belly will disappear?' Granny asked with a twinkle in her eye.

Henry shook his head.

'Then the leftovers won't either. I bet Greta would be happy not to have to cook one night this week. She has had quite a crowd at the restaurant every single night.'

5. Babysitting

Grace

With the boy safely at his Granny's for the night, the black wolf returned to her pack. All the pups yipped and ran to greet her. For a while she fooled around, letting them wrestle her to the ground and jump all over her. When she got tired, she nudged the pups toward their parents. The alpha female dealt with her two prancing boys rather well.

The pack had been wary when she had first appeared. As well they should be. It was rare for wolf packs to accept outsiders. Not that she had known this.

Two years ago, she hadn't given a second thought to wolves or how they communicated or their habits, except when she had read Henry his bedtime stories. Living with the pack was an eye-opener. How they cared for each other, how the leaders delegated the leading except when they could sense danger and then the alphas would steer the pack away from it. Like a few months ago, when they had narrowly escaped overstepping the boundaries of their hunting grounds and the alphas had sensed a rival pack nearby.

It was the pups that had saved the day when she had tried and failed to make it on her own for weeks after she had been turned. She must have sent out some sort of I-love-pups vibe because first she found a lost pup and when she took him back to the pack, the other fur-balls ran to her and their rescued sibling, nearly falling over themselves, ignoring the growls and stillness of the grown-ups. A hesitant approach and a sniffing appraisal by their mother later, and the black she-wolf had become the designated babysitter ever since.

She and the crows.

Yes, who knew that wolves and crows led a symbiotic life? The crows liked to hang out by the caves and gobble up the nutritious wolf feces, occasionally snapping at the pups. Their version of playing. Even in winter, when the wolves went hungry, never had she seen them kill a crow for food. The wolves would rather eat mice, rats, beavers, even vegetables they could dig up, but they didn't touch their crows. It could very well be that those nosy buggers tasted like hell, but she thought having them as a free warning system was more important.

Wolves would never kill their guardians.

Guardians.

The wolf didn't have the energy to even grind her teeth.

Guardians were the reason she had landed this job. Guardian angels to be precise. And yes, she still thought of this as a job. A protracted save, even when nobody was in any particular danger and she had no idea when the gig would end. Quite the contrary, she had been told by Gabriel, the Bossest of them all that this was permanent.

She put a paw out and touched the lightest one of the pups who was starting to annoy the alpha. He quieted and crawled to her on his belly.

Peter

PETER LAY ON HIS STOMACH in the tall grass. He congratulated himself for choosing a hiding place high up and downwind.

The wolves didn't seem to be aware of him. Only the black one perked her ears up and looked in his direction, but she didn't alert the others.

That's right. I'm no threat.

In two years, he had finally mastered following them, unseen.

He only wanted to watch. Learn. Remember. Analyze.

She had led him straight to them as if she had meant to.

Her not reacting to his presence meant she wanted him to watch.

Did she mean to show me that she is happy in her new life? Tending to the pups of others instead of raising her own child?

The silver-coated one looked like he was the leader and the white wolf was his mate. The alphas. Who had had two new pups this spring, but only one survived. The alpha male lazily looked on as a young wolf approached the pups and playfully nipped at one of them. The light-grey pup yipped happily and bit back. The teenager who had himself been a pup only last year fell backwards and turned his belly up, demonstrating defeat. The lighter pup towered over his elder, looking proud.

The huntsman smiled.

What are elder brothers for but to teach through play how victory feels?

Grace

THE BLACK WOLF GOT up and coughed, once.

The pups perked up their ears as she trotted off toward the woods.

Let another lesson begin.

The black wolf sighed. She prayed a time would come when the lesson would be that humans and wolves could co-exist without fear, which was making life on either side more fretful than it needed to be. That time had not arrived yet, given that the huntsman was using corpses of wolves who had died of more or less natural causes to make the villagers believe he had killed a wolf every now and then.

6. Fairytales

At the hut

With the boy fed, bathed and in bed, Granny pulled out a weathered leather-bound book and asked, 'Which story shall I tell you tonight?'

'About Red Riding Hood and the wolf who loved pancakes, pleeeease, Granny!' Henry pleaded and Granny wondered how someone who had never seen Shrek could do the Puss in Boots eyes so impeccably.

Grizelda rolled her eyes. 'I know it's your favorite, but I've read it to you a thousand times.'

Henry nodded, smiling. 'I know, but I love how the wolf can't make pancakes and Granny and Red teach him.'

'Henry, you do know that wolves don't usually eat pancakes? A normal wolf might prefer to eat you instead?' Granny inclined her head and tried to sound serious.

The boy nodded. 'I know. But not my wolf. She loooooves pancakes.'

'Are you sure?'

The boy scrambled up to see out the window. A white plate gleamed in the moonlight. 'Quite sure. She ate them all.'

Granny looked out at the full moon and then at the plate. 'She did?'

The boy looked thoughtful. 'Do you think we made her?'

'Made her?'

'Made her like pancakes. You told the story a thousand times and I believed the story and then a wolf appeared who likes pancakes.'

The witch looked at him and tilted her head. 'You think I told you the story about the wolf who liked pancakes so many times that it made such a wolf appear?'

The boy nodded.

'Life imitating art,' the witch mumbled. 'Why would it?'

'Why not? Maybe the story just needed someone to believe in it?' The boy smiled.

'Well, the only way to try out that theory is to tell you a new story and see what happens,' the witch suggested.

Henry's eyes lit up.

Granny opened the tattered leather tome. 'Right, let's choose another one of your mother's fairytales, shall we, Red?'

Henry snuck his feet under the wool blanket and hugged his teddy bear tight.

'Three Rocking Pigs.' Granny chuckled. 'Oh, I remember what Grace did with this one...'

The boy snuggled closer.

Three Rocking Pigs

Far, far away in the woods there once lived an old woman, who was childless. Going about the neighboring farms, the woman gathered three pigs. The first one she bought. The second one she borrowed and the third one she got for free, seeing as it had a crippled hoof and would have otherwise been eaten.

The old woman raised these pigs as if they were her own children. She fed them, petted them, read them fairytales at bedtime and even gave them names - Naf-Naf, Nif-Nif and Nuf-Nuf, because they made such adorable noises.

Yule-time came. Food supplies were scarce and the old woman thought, however am I going to feed my piglets? She could manage with peppermint tea, but the pigs would want proper food. She considered sending the pigs to help out at one of the farms.

Nuf-Nuf overheard the woman muttering to herself about these things and went and told his brothers: 'Brothers, it seems that mother is very much worried about us and the hunger has taken the last remnants of her mind. She wants us to go and serve at farms just before Yule. In winter, the servants have nothing to do, but we can well be coaxed into a pot-roast, especially if the farmer has no pigs or if he's sorry to slaughter his own. Then they wouldn't have to pay us either. Let's go into the wide world and seek our fortune elsewhere. Better than ending up as Christmas dinner.' His brothers agreed and they fled into the woods at night.

The winter was cold and the night was dark. In all the kerfuffle, the brothers ended up scurrying everywhichway. Naf-Naf went East, Nif-Nif went South and Nuf-Nuf ended up going West.

Naf-Naf found discarded rags near one of the villages and donned them. Walking on his hind legs took some getting used to, but he managed. With his hat pulled over his nose and a triangular scarf shielding the bottom half of his face he stepped in front of a caravan of merchants. He survived. Having checked his pants were still clean, he shouted: 'Woodchips or your life!' The merchants laughed at his *costume, took mercy and gave the lug-of- a-pig a pile of straw. Naf-Naf was content, built himself a small house on the outskirts of the village and became a pig farming consultant.*

Nif-Nif made it to the river. He was just thinking how to get across when he saw a raft near the shore. Instead of continuing his journey, he dismantled the raft and built himself a house by the river. In time, he found more wooden boards and made a new raft and started ferrying people and animals across. Only the very fortunate few knew how to swim in the olden days, you see.

Nuf-Nuf roamed the woods the longest. Starvation was staring him in his snout and his lame leg was aching something awful, yet the woods grew deeper and darker. One stormy night he arrived upon a stone shack, ill-lit by candle light. Nuf-Nuf remembered an ancient fairytale that the old woman had read to them. He howled like a bobcat, growled like a dog, squealed like a pig, crooned like a rooster and kicked like a mule, but when the inhabitants refused to leave, he hummed a few bars from a shark tale the old woman used to read them and opened the door with a squeak. Upon hearing this, the robbers whose house it was ran screaming into the night forest and never came back. The forest was by the marshes, perhaps that's why. Nuf-Nuf made himself comfortable in his newly acquired house.

When the old woman went to rouse the piglets in the morning and found them gone, she realized that her dear piggies had spared her the struggle of feeding them and had sought their fortunes elsewhere. Greatly saddened that hunger and fear for the safety of their lives had driven her precious pigs from their home, the old woman went to the village witch and asked her to make it so that she would never have to go hungry again during her life-time. The witch smiled and asked: 'Are you sure, love?' The old woman nodded and the witch gave her a potion and told her to drink it before bedtime.

The old woman did as she was told and woke up as a wolf the next morning. After all, there had been no agreement that the life-time had to be the one of a human being.

The wolf looked about in the house and got scared.

She! A wolf! In a human house!

As a wolf, the old woman didn't remember anything of her previous life. The wolf jumped through the window and into the yard where it sniffed the air. The air smelled delicious. Mmmm... Like tasty little piglets.

She followed their scent to the barn where the pigs had slept, in their little bedsides, on their soft strawsies, near their tiny troughsies. When the wolf didn't find the pigs in the barn, she started sniffing around - where had her tasty meal gone?

The first pig smelled like Christmas roast with plums and apples. The indents of his feet were also the deepest. Big, juicy, fat pig! The salivating wolf ran into the forest, turned East and reached the village at the edge of which Naf-Naf had built his hut of straw.

Having reached the straw hut, the wolf howled with glee. Naf-Naf heard her and ran away from the hut. He had received a letter from Nif-Nif, which said that his brother now lived by the river and that Naf-Naf should visit, and Naf-Naf decided now would be an opportune time to see his middle brother. The pig struck a deal with one of the merchants and secured himself passage on a cart.

When the wolf realized that the biggest pig was not coming home and there was no point in keeping watch there, she howled once in frustration, then exhaled...and the straw hut flew to the four winds. The wolf enquired here and there from the wild folk and a woodpecker told her that he had seen a huge fat talking pig in one of the merchants' caravans. The woodpecker even pointed the wolf in the direction of the river, where the cart had gone.

When the wolf reached the river, from afar she saw two pigs entering a hut made of wooden planks. Two whole pigs! Two! The wolf started howling again from sheer joy. The pigs heard her and Nif-Nif said: 'Listen, Naf-Naf, I know you just got here, but Nuf-Nuf wrote me that he lives in a forest, in a stone hut. I'm a bit scared of the wolf. There have never been wolves afoot near the river before. Let's see, maybe it will leave. If it does not, then I know how to get across the river and we'll go visit with Nuf-Nuf for a little while.' And so, it was decided.

The wolf waited and waited by the door. The pigs waited and waited on the other side of it. In the meantime, a whole bunch of people who all wanted to get across gathered on the riverbank...

GRANNY GLANCED AT THE sleeping boy, skipped a few pages to the end and finished with 'The wolf made the deal with the pigs, yadda-yadda, and in eight years' time the pigs took on another wolf, from the old she-wolf's only litter. Because pigs live fifteen to twenty years while wolves only live six to eight. Thus, came true the old woman's wish that she would never have to go hungry again during her lifetime.'

The old woman closed the book, blew the candle out, and pulled the blanket over the boy who was already fast asleep, clutching his teddy-bear.

7. Mirror, Mirror

The next morning Grizelda was up long before Red. He fell out of bed and headed for the common room with a huge yawn. Henry was about to utter 'What's for breakfast?' when he noticed Granny twirling around the hut, singing and swaying her hips.

'What'cha doing?' Henry asked and Granny froze mid-sway.

'My, what big eyes you have, Red,' Granny said.

'The better to see you with. Were you singing?'

'My, what big ears you have, Red.' Granny smirked.

'The better to hear you with. I also have big teeth, Granny, but I'm not a wolf, I'm not going to eat you.' Henry laughed.

'What are those?' The boy pointed to the two pieces of white mate- rial nestled in Granny's ears.

Granny sighed. 'Ear buds. To listen to music. Contraband from the Warriors. You know, the mysterious warlords up North?'

'Who is playing it? Where are they? Are they hiding?' The boy looked around.

'No. Someone played the music a long, long time ago and someone else recorded it. I'm listening to a recording that this thing...' Granny showed him a small flat pink rectangle with a round button in the middle, '...can play for me.'

'This tiny thing has music in it? But I can't hear it. I only heard your singing. You have a lovely singing voice, Granny.'

'I used to be in an all-girl band. When I was young.'

'You?'

'You wouldn't believe the half of it,' Grizelda muttered.

'I bet you were the prettiest girl,' the boy said.

'Flatterer. Do you want to hear the music I was listening to?'

The boy nodded.

The woman lifted the devices out of her ears and into the boy's.

His eyes lit up and his mouth fell open as he heard the percussions egg the piano on and on until the sax overrode all the instruments with its slow sorrowful cry that faded into the *tippi-tap* of the piano keys imitating rain.

Granny gave it a few more minutes before she asked, 'Like it?'

The boy looked up, spell-bound. 'What is this music?'

'Jazz, baby, this is jazz.'

With breakfast done, the boy started gathering up his teddy bear and the picnic basket.

The witch put the food into the basket and weighed it. 'Not too heavy. You can carry it, you're a strong boy. The wolf can help.'

Except the wolf was nowhere to be seen. Granny blamed it on the pancakes - the poor animal was probably suffering indigestion from human food.

Granny caught Henry by the scruff on his way out. 'Red, go straight, remember? Stay on the path, you hear.'

'I know.' The five-year old scanned the underbrush.

'No, listen, it's the full moon, you need to stay on the path.' The witch raised the boy's chin. 'The path, Henry. No flower-picking. No squirrel-chasing. No nothing. Got it?'

The boy nodded, looking serious. 'Papa said the same thing yesterday.'

'And there is a good reason for it.'

'Is that because the paths switch around?'

'What do you mean switch around, dear?' the witch asked.

'Well, once, I stepped off the path to pet a hedgehog and when I did the oak tree was on my left, but when I turned back, the oak tree was on my left again, although it should have been on my right. It had switched around. The trees in your forest, they walk about, don't they?'

Granny eyed the boy. 'Oh, I hope not.'

'Is it the trees or the paths that sneak around, Granny?'

'You know, sneaking around is exactly what I've suspected they do. That's why I sometimes have to go and get my visitors from the woods where they have gotten lost. Like that one time, when I knew Betty was coming to visit in the morning and it was already past noon and she wasn't here. I looked in my mirror,' the witch pointed to the half-shrouded bronze mirror next to her stove.

'And there she was - sitting underneath that huge oak tree. She told me that no matter what path she took, all the paths led back to the oak.'

'But they don't, do they? If you managed to rescue her?'

The old woman nodded. 'There is only one direct path from the village to my hut, one direct path through the forest from your house to my hut and one direct path from the oak to my home. All the other paths loop back to the oak. That's why it's important that you stick to the path when you come visit me, okay?'

'Did you make the looping paths, Granny?'

'No, I did not.'

'Who did?'

'I don't know, dear. But because of those loops, I did make the direct paths, though.'

'How?' Henry was all ears.

'I'm a witch, don't you know?' The old woman winked.

'Okay but HOW did you make them? What did you do?' Henry scrunched his brows.

Granny shrugged. 'I just believed my legs would get me home, that's all. I have a feeling that people get lost when they start believing they are lost. Belief is a powerful thing, Red. But you...' she tousled his hair, '...you stay on the path. Even if you are clever enough to continue on the right path despite the trees moving around.'

'Oh, it wasn't me who was clever. It was the wolf. She appeared on the road and stared at me until I followed, and it was in the right direction.' Henry waved at the bushes.

'Your pancake-eating wolf?' The witch crouched down to the boy's level and got another nod.

Granny patted the boy's head. 'Seems that anything is possible when you are around. Will you introduce me to your wolf?' the witch asked, stealing glances at the underbrush. 'I need to have a talk with her.'

'I will, Granny, but right now, I have to go, she's waiting for me to go back.'

'How do you know she is waiting for you, Red?'

'She's right there.' The boy pointed to the ferns.

Granny nodded. 'Alright. But for my ease of mind, will you give your wolf some food?'

'I'll give her one of the veal cutlets on the way back. She likes those.'

'I hope she doesn't like little boys,' she mumbled and waved a finger at the underbrush. 'Get him home safe or else you'll have me to answer to, wolf!' the witch said sternly. 'And come back for that chat.'

'Granny!' Henry said, looking dismayed.

'Oh, don't you worry. If she likes you, she won't mind my manners.'

Not for the first time since she'd been stuck in Magic Kingdom thirty-six years ago the witch itched to flip out her phone and dial someone. The huntsman in this instance.

As the boy walked down the path, what seemed like a large black dog appeared at his side. The witch hurried back into her hut.

'I might not have a cell phone, but I have something better. Mirror, mirror on the wall, show me the forest, path and all,' she told her bronze mirror, freeing it from its linen confines.

8. Lies and Reasons

Peter

The huntsman spotted the familiar black snout only a few feet away as he watched his son coming out of the woods, dragging the wicker basket.

Peter walked over to ease his load. 'Henry, get inside. Now.'

Peter scanned the woods for her, but the wolf was already gone. She was following Henry a bit too close for comfort.

Peter sighed.

Sooner or later, I will have to tell Henry the truth.

Or a part of it.

When Peter went back inside, he saw that Henry had already set the round table in the middle of their sparse abode, using the wooden plates and cutlery, remnants from their old home. 'Henry.'

The boy turned around, holding a huge slice of cherry pie. Both the boy and Grace had the habit of starting the meal with sweets.

'Yes, Papa?'

Peter crouched down to Henry's level. 'Have you ever wondered why I chose to be a huntsman and Hans a woodcutter?'

The boy shook his head, careful not to get blobs of cherry onto his shirt.

Peter sighed and sat down.

'Just before your Mama was taken from us...' Peter said, looking into eyes that radiated innocence, 'we took in Greta and Hans...'

'They haven't always lived with us?' Henry asked, taking another bite and Peter shook his head.

'For a while, they lived with their godmother, Melisandra.'

'The Fairy Godmother? The one that got Ella her happily ever after? That Fairy Godmother?'

'The Fairy Godmother. She had to be away a lot and so we all decided that it would be better if Hans and Greta lived with us.'

Henry scrunched his brows. 'But now Greta lives by herself in the village. In the house where we used to live. And she runs The Duchess.'

'And we live here. We moved into the woods after Mama was... taken. I couldn't keep living in the village amongst all the pitying stares, not that I'd expect you to understand.' Peter sighed. 'Right about the same time, there were sightings of a wolf and everybody in the village was afraid the wolves would go after their sheep. The village didn't have a huntsman, so I volunteered, even though my acquaintance with a rifle up to that point had been minimal, at best.'

'You didn't know how to hunt? You lied?' The boy gaped, almost spilling the plate of vegetables Greta had prepared for them before she had left.

Peter nodded, taking the plate, but picked out only a few boiled carrots.

'I learnt by myself, shooting at different unmoving and then moving targets in the woods. I just told them part of the truth - that I could shoot, which I could, and that I was moving into the woods to keep everyone safe. But I moved as much to get away from everyone.'

'I understand, Papa. You didn't want everyone coming by our house and talking about Mama. You just wanted to be by yourself and think happy thoughts about Mama. The wolf just happened.' Henry, done with the pie, reached for a gob of mashed potatoes.

Peter looked up in surprise. 'That's right. The wolf just happened. I became a huntsman because the wolf happened. And I'm glad I did. I have learnt quite a lot about the wolves during the past two years.'

Images of following the pack and the black wolf surfaced in Peter's mind.

'And Hans?'

'What about Hans?' Peter blinked the memories away.

'Is he a woodcutter because that is his magic?'

Peter scratched his chin. 'What do you mean?'

'When he takes up his axe, it always zings. And it always cuts the wood, neat. It never cuts Hans.'

Peter remembered seeing the logs arranging themselves into a neat pile and dismissing it as a hallucination. 'He's really careful with his axe. Respectful, even.'

Henry nodded. 'I've seen how Hans talks to the trees he picks to cut down. He always promises to plant a new tree. And after, a new sapling grows next to the old stump in months.'

'That's because of the good soil, he picks the right place where to plant.' Peter looked down on his empty plate.

'But once, the tree, the soil and that patch of the forest were all dead and a new tree grew anyway,' Henry said. 'Remember that time when Hans helped Greta make the sign for our restaurant and flowers sprang from it in winter? He made the sign come to life!'

'Henry...' Peter admonished.

'I'm telling you, Papa.' The little boy looked up. 'When Mama left... When I was sad, Hans made me a toy soldier and when one day I couldn't find him, he said maybe he came to life and sneaked off into the woods. That's magic, isn't it, Papa?' Henry looked intently at his father.

Peter sighed. 'Well, he never gets lost in the woods, even at night, that's for sure.'

Henry smiled.

Peter ruffled the boy's hair. 'I guess you can call some of it magic. I would just call it being one with nature, being good with his hands and having great orientation skills.'

Henry nodded. 'You don't believe in magic. That's okay. Not everybody does. Granny said so.'

'Did she now?' Peter smiled.

'Mama told her she doesn't believe in magic either. And Granny does.'

'Yes, I guess your Mama didn't believe in magic,' Peter mused.

'Sometimes magic believes in you. That's what Granny says,' Henry said.

Peter glanced out the window. 'You could say that again where your Mama is concerned.'

'Magic happened to Mama?' Henry's eyes goggled.

'You know those shoes your big sister Ella keeps telling you about?'

'The ones Mellie loaned her and then took back?'

'The ones Mellie *took*, yes. Although she would not be happy about you calling her Mellie. She likes Melisandra.' The man ruffled his son's hair. 'These are magic shoes. It was your Mama's fairy godmother who gave them to Mama who gave them to Ella.' Peter winked.

'Mama gave those shoes to Ella? Not Aunt Mellie?'

Peter nodded.

'Mama had a real fairy for a godmother?'

'Yup. And you are magic, too. Grace and I, Mama and Papa... We tried and tried and tried and then we had you, which WAS magic. And then we came to live here where there are fairy godmothers and kings and queens and Ella became a princess, which was also a little magic. So, you can say magic kept happening around Mama. Some would even say she made some of that magic happen herself, like with Ella. Even when she didn't believe in it. Even in the end...'

'In the end? What happened? Something magical?'

'An angel took her,' Peter said quietly, rising, plate in hand.

'Mama is with the angels now?' Henry asked.

Peter nodded, turning away so his son wouldn't see the hope on his face. 'And you are all I have of Mama now, so you need to be careful,' he said, gruffness creeping into his voice.

Henry nodded and ran up to hug Peter tight.

'I'm talking about the wolf, Henry. You need to be careful,' Peter said, crouching down.

The boy stiffened for a second. 'You know about her? How?'

'I saw her following you from Granny's just now.'

'She is just looking after me. She's not dangerous. You don't have to shoot her dead!' Henry pleaded.

Peter sighed. 'I know. She's one of the good ones. If you trust her, I trust her. But I'm still going to keep my eye on you two.'

Henry hugged him again. 'Sure, I'll tell her you said so.'

When Peter raised an eyebrow, Henry shrugged. 'Hans talks to trees and axes, why can't I talk to a wolf?'

'Does it talk back?' Peter asked.

'Sometimes it nods and shakes its head when I ask it questions,' Henry said. 'Sometimes she laughs. She coughs, but it sounds like a laugh to me.'

Peter smiled, the motion unfamiliar across the last few years. 'Yes, wolves have ways to communicate. You know, people have lots of misconceptions about wolves. Probably because of all the horrible fairytales they have been told growing up. Wolves eating children and their grandmothers. Stalking a goat mama and breaking into her house to eat her seven kids.'

'Stealing sheep and goats from the pastures,' Henry added.

'No, that they do, but only when other food is scarce in their area. Why would they want to upset humans who have rifles and can hunt them down, hmm…?' Peter inclined his head. 'I took up being a huntsman so I could keep the humans from killing every wolf in the area. I have used dead wolves to fool the villagers and I don't know, maybe the wolves are not happy about that. I wish there was a way to agree this was the best way we can co-exist peacefully.'

'Maybe you could talk to them?' Henry offered, helping to clear the table.

'How?' Peter asked.

'You could talk to the black wolf and she could talk to the others,' Henry said.

'If only it was that simple, Henry. If only it was that simple,' Peter said and looked out the window. Somewhere in that underbrush, their wolf was waiting. There were so many things he wanted to talk to her about. Human-wolf relations were not the topmost on his list.

9. The Potion

At the hut

Sticking some bread onto a knife, the witch scanned the underbrush. When she found what she was looking for, she smirked and ambled down the steps of her house, across the meadow and toward the forest and its ferns. At the edge of the woods the witch hitched up her colorful skirts, knelt and held her knife out.

The wolf sniffed at the bread and took a step forward.

'Say, you're not the wolf who slaughtered those sheep two years ago?' the witch asked.

The wolf shook her head.

'Just wanted to be sure. I'm glad we got that settled. Are you hungry? Try this!' The witch held the knife out by its pearl handle as far out as she could stretch her arm.

The wolf took another step and carefully closed its jaws around the bread, then slipped the piece off.

'You're familiar with knives. Good.' The old woman sat down cross-legged and mumbled, 'This better work.'

The wolf swallowed. Her eyes flashed purple and her paws started sliding in different directions.

'That's right. You lie down now.' The witch smiled and fumbled for something behind her.

The wolf didn't want to lie down. Instead, she started crawling back into the forest, limping and scratching at her skin.

'Wait! Don't make this any more difficult than it has to be,' the witch said.

Disoriented and in pain, the wolf let out a howl.

'*Shhh*! Do you want the villagers to come running? Come here!' Grizelda gave the animal's backside a hefty push toward her hut, muttering, 'If you stray

33

too far and faint, how am I going to drag you to the hut? You weigh a ton. And stop resisting, it'll be over quicker.'

Eventually the wolf lay motionless at the witch's feet, her head on the first stair. In a purple flash, she was gone.

A naked human lay on the ground instead.

The old woman took a throw off her shoulder and spread it over the body.

'Ouch. Quite some potion,' rasped the woman under the throw. 'Now I know what the Sea Witch gave Ariel. Got any clothes, Grizelda?'

The old woman asked, 'Do I know you?'

'You used to.' A head poked out from under the throw.

Grizelda frowned. 'Your face... It looks familiar and yet... younger. You were tailing Henry... I should have known.' The witch sighed. 'Get dressed, Grace, then we'll talk.'

'It's a good thing the potion meant for me also works on you,' she mumbled.

The younger woman stumbled up the steps and into the hut, hugging the throw close. Minutes later, she re-appeared in the doorway, sporting a skirt that was too long for her. Grace smiled shyly and ruffled her short jet-black hair.

The witch beamed. 'As good as new.' She narrowed her eyes. 'Come to think of it, even better than new. You... all of you... looks younger than I remember from two years ago! Why, I wouldn't say you were a day older than twenty-five! And rather familiar, but not as Ella's stepmother, although I can't quite put my finger on it...'

'Good to see you too, Grizelda,' Grace said. 'How did you know the wolf might be human?'

'You read enough Russian fairytales, you see the signs of someone being enchanted... or cursed - depends how you look at it.'

'Is this permanent?' Grace asked, running her hand down the colorful skirt Grizelda had lent her, jotting an errant ink-black lock behind her ear.

'Sadly, no. You'll change back in a day or so. Now go hide, I have a visitor coming along any minute now,' said the witch, pointing toward the bedroom.

10. Wishes

When the lady who had come for her pregnancy-preserving herbs and a hearty chat had gone, the witch hollered at her bedroom, 'The coast is clear, you can come out now!'

The wolf stuck out her snout.

'You've turned back again? But it has barely been an hour! Bad luck, old gal.' The witch clucked her tongue.

The wolf whined.

'Oh, no. Don't you wish it wasn't so.' Grizelda wagged her finger at the wolf. 'Let me tell you about wishing. I'm the horrible warning for why you should never wish things were not how they are. Most importantly, you should never ever make a wish in front of a goddess,' Grizelda said. 'I'm the one to talk. I swear, I'm not as crazy as the goddess who granted me my wish. But I have tried my best to avoid people and their wishes for the past thirty-six years. And still they come to the woods to seek me out.' She shook her head. 'But no wishing for you, missy! You've had enough bad luck to last you several lifetimes, it seems.'

The wolf perked up her ears.

'Oh, what's that about goddesses, you ask?' The witch chuckled. 'Well, the one who granted me my errant wish was the Goddess of Fate. And while I might not look all golden or glorious or eternally young, you are looking at a Goddess of Luck. A temporary Goddess of Luck. I was originally the new Goddess of Change, but Della and I switched. Never mind. For now, I'm Luck. At your service.' The self-professed goddess bowed and winced. 'Well, not really. No wishes!' She pointed a finger like an angry schoolmarm and straightened up, clutching her back. 'Damnation, I was hoping to get to be eternally young when I found out I'm the new vanguard, but oh, well... Time does not work well with me, not in this dimension.'

The wolf stood up, prancing on her feet.

Grizelda straightened, clutching her back and said through gritted teeth, 'No wishes!'

The wolf tilted her head.

'Why am I so anti-wishes, you ask? Let me tell you.' Grizelda sat down, easing into her only comfortable armchair. 'There I was, twenty-five and living a life of luxury in Moscow, Earth dimension. No husband, no kids, free to dart all around the globe whenever I pleased with just one fly in the ointment. An amazingly endowed,' the witch sighed, 'but sadly, a married lover. On one of those visits to see a dear friend in London, I wished to experience a real life, have a family, kids and grandkids of my own, but without the memory of cheating on Oleg - the man I was with, or rather am still with in my other life.'

'Ma-ri-na.' The wolf barked.

'What did you say?' The woman did a double take. 'How do you know my Earthen name?'

'I. Am. Grace.' The wolf barked.

'I know that.'

'I. Am. Grace.' The wolf looked Grizelda in the eye.

'This is sounding a lot like I am Groot,' the witch mumbled. 'Am I supposed to guess what that means?'

'Del-la's Grace.'

'Della? How do you know my university friend from London?' Grizelda's eyes goggled. 'You're Della's Grace?!? Della's room-mate Grace? From London?' The witch wolf-whistled. 'I thought there was something familiar about your youthful self. That one time that I saw you in London, you were a stick insect. At least in the Magic Kingdom you filled out nicely and now you're back to being a stick insect again! Wow, the world is small. No, I stand corrected. The universe and all its dimensions are way too intertwined, if both of us from Earth end up together in the Magic Kingdom.' The old woman laughed.

The wolf put her snout into Grizelda's outstretched palm.

'It's not fair that I'm old and you've been turned into a wolf, but at least now I have someone to talk to about Earth!' The witch winked. 'Now, where was I?'

'You. Came. Here.'

'Ah, yes. As soon as I had spoken my wish out loud, Faith, the Olden Goddess of Fate laughed and said "Your wish is my command!" and sent me to this dimension! Forty years without parole. Forty years! Seriously.'

'Can. You. Go. Back?'

'Not before the forty years are up. Believe me, I tried. No such luck.' The old woman looked sour. 'Pun NOT intended.'

'You. Got. Your. Wish.'

The old woman sighed. 'I know. I've lived a lifetime in the Magic Kingdom in the past thirty-six years. Got here, changed my Russian name to something witchy. In Russian, the word sounds like someone who gnaws at something. Grizelda.' The witch stretched her name into a growl. 'I felt like gnawing on something alright, so that's the name I told to the first person from the village who asked me for it and the moniker stuck. Then I got Mellie. Got grandkids and even one great-grandkid, courtesy of Ella and her prince. I got my wish. Only four more years to go.'

The wolf put her paw on the witch's hand.

'The thing is, none of this will matter. When I return back home, I will have missed one day. One. Time runs differently in this Magic Kingdom of ours. It's the fairytales. Time is supposed to run differently here as the tales are made, remembered and remade. When I go home, a day will have passed - or so Fate said - and I will be young and beautiful again. Nothing will have changed back home. Except I will have become forty years the wiser.'

'How?'

'When my time in this fairytale world is up, all I have to do is drink one dose from that vial,' Grizelda pointed at the bottle, 'and I'll turn back into my young, hot, twenty-five-year-old self and be transported back to my previous life. I guess there'll have to be some extra instructions or I have to take it on the fortieth anniversary of my internment here or something.'

The wolf cocked her head.

'How do I know?' Grizelda pursed her lips. 'On the first night I was here, this vial appeared with a writing "Drink me when you want to go back in 40 years." Bloody stealing from Alice in Wonderland, if you ask me. Naturally, I took a good swig, hoping to go back immediately. No such luck. I did lose a few wrinkles, but stayed put. Writing appeared on the side of the vial. "You wanted to live in a fairytale, so here you are - see you in 40 years." I got so angry. I don't remember much of the week that followed. I do remember giving birth to a daughter nine months later.'

'Mel-lie.' The wolf barked with a glint in her eyes.

'Yes, Mellie. I still don't know whose daughter she is. Maybe she is Oleg's and maybe she is the spawn of the handsome rogue who passed by and plied me with booze that first week I got here,' the witch said, looking grim. 'For a week I waited for Fate to appear and tell me it was all a stupid prank and that I could go home. But nobody came out of the bushes and yelled "Surprise! Have you had enough of this yet?" A charming silver-haired fox of a man happened to pass by the hut and I thought it would be a good idea if we got horribly, horribly drunk. He was gone in the morning, before I had woken up. I don't even know his name. But the goddess was true to her word – if something did happen, I do not remember it. So, I don't recall cheating on Oleg as if it never happened.'

The wolf nudged the witch's palm and the old woman patted her head.

'I know, I know. I shouldn't complain. It has been an interesting experience, mind you. I've been feared and hated while all I do is help women and men on occasion to get exactly what they want with herbal remedies and sometimes a few choice Russian words aimed to point out their shortcomings. Which they always mistake for spells, I swear!' The old woman laughed. 'Ten years ago, my own daughter spread lies about how I am a cannibalistic witch who almost ate her own grandkids.'

The wolf growled.

'Yes. Luckily you sorted that out by telling Hans and Greta about what really happened. But then you disappeared and nobody knew what had happened to you. I guess I know now. In any case, thank you for setting the record straight. That I didn't try to eat the twins, that I took them in when Mellie had kicked them out into the wintry woods.' Grizelda shook the vial with the purple liquid. 'I guess if this was meant for me, that would explain why the effect wears off more quickly on those who were not the intended recipients. Sorry, hon.'

'How. Long.'

'For me?' The witch asked. 'Oh, a day or so. At least until sundown. Hours.'

'Show. Me.'

'Oh, why not!' Grizelda winked, unscrewed the cap from the bottle and poured a little of the liquid in there.

'Bottoms up!' she said and down the hatch it went.

The old woman held on to the table and started coughing violently.

On the first cough, her wispy grey hair turned pitch black and curled into tighter ringlets.

On the second cough, her floppy stomach disappeared, her boobs filled out as her shoulders pulled back and she grew a few inches.

On the third cough, her wrinkled skin was pulled taunt.

'Damn, you'd think it would hurt less the second time,' Grizelda said, still gripping the table. 'Ten years ago, I decided to treat myself to a vainglorious birthday party. It hurt just as bad then as it did now, which is why I don't usually touch the stuff.' She fingered her saggy dress. 'I need new clothes. And a drink. Do you want one?' She motioned at the bottle.

The wolf eyed the bottle and the woman, then nodded.

Grizelda poured out a capful and said, 'Open wide.'

The wolf did as she was told.

The witch threw the contents of the cap into the wolf's maw and took a few steps back.

11. Trading Stories

At the hut

As Grace was getting changed, the former Granny prepared tea.
'We look the same age now,' Grace said. 'So, what do I call you now, Grizelda, Marina, Goddess or Granny?'

'Nobody knows I'm a goddess and I'd like to keep it that way. It would be just plain weird if you called me Granny. I don't feel like Marina here. No, let that be reserved for Earth.' The woman waved her hand and whispered to the table cloth. Cinnamon rolls appeared next to the steaming teapot. 'Witch is... not quite true, despite some magical artefacts I found in the hut. I'm more of a herbalist, to be honest. I guess Grizelda is fine, since this,' she motioned at her twenty-something body, 'is temporary. Feel free to call me Granny, if it's in front of the others. But you'd need to be rehabilitated into our little village society before you can call me anything. Any plans?'

Grace laughed, her voice throaty. 'Straight to the point, as always... Grizelda.'

'What's the point of dallying? I like straight arrows.' Grizelda shrugged.

'Yes, indeed.' Grace chuckled. 'Now I understand why Ella had the most inordinate amount of luck imaginable,' she said, taking a seat at the table. 'She can create opportunities out of nothing. If you're the new Goddess of Luck, bits of your powers must have trickled down to your granddaughter. Even if you try your damnedest not to exercise those powers.'

Grizelda eyed her magic dinner cloth and her mirror. 'You know, me not using my powers of Luck doesn't mean I don't attract it. I guess being a goddess does come with some perks.'

Grace laughed again. 'You know, I would never have recognized you as Della's Marina, if you hadn't told me,' she said. 'When Peter, Henry and I arrived here, you were already thirty years older than when I last saw you. And back on Earth, Peter and I were so caught up in each other and with trying to have a baby for more than ten years, that I completely missed how you fared in London.'

'So, when I met you in the Magic Kingdom you were about fifteen years older since I last saw you in London?' Grizelda *tsk-tsk*-ed and poured them some tea. 'Fate stuck me here when I was visiting Della. You and I had just met.'

'At that time, I hadn't even met Peter yet,' Grace said.

'For you, our meeting was fifteen years ago. For me, it was thirty-six years ago. You have seen ten years happen on Earth since we first met. I haven't lived those ten years yet as I'll be going back into the day after we met,' Grizelda said.

'It's all because Time flows differently here.' Grace nodded.

'Although it might flow differently, I've still felt and lived every single day of those thirty-six years.' Grizelda winced. 'I swear, if I could give Fate her comeuppance, I will.'

'You want revenge? Why? You only have four more years to go,' Grace said and it earned her a scowl. 'Well, if you were meant to have Mellie and she was meant to have kids, your grandkids, then what do you want revenge for? You got your wish. Forty years makes sense - it fits an entire life.'

'Yes, but what I meant was to live my own life, the one that I had, out as an ethereal, otherworldly fairytale, where Oleg wasn't married or, rather, where he was married to ME and where I could be wise enough to make good choices so that everything would go my way,' Grizelda said wistfully.

'Well, you still can, don't you think? Here, you got to live out several fairytales, not just one. When your time is up, you will be restored to who you were plus one day, but with decades of life experience, which has to count as wisdom and voilà, you will get to live out yet another fairytale life!'

'And the wisdom I take from Hans and Greta's fairytale is what – don't eat children?' Grizelda said darkly. 'Or in my case – don't piss off your daughter or she'll make your grandkids hate you? Or in the case of Ella – whore around as much as you like, you'll still end up with the prince?' The witch *huffed*. 'Besides, how am I going to leave my family? I don't know if they can come with me and if they can, can you just picture me back, in the glitzy Moscow life, twenty-five and with a daughter who is older than me and already has one grandkid? Unlikely.' She poured them more tea. 'Not that Mellie would ever admit to being a grandmother,' she mumbled and sighed. 'It feels good to talk it out for a change, but I could still strangle Fate!'

'She would strangle you right back for not using her assumed name.' Grace smiled.

'It's Faith, darling, if you don't mind!' The duo said in unison and fell about laughing.

'I used to love Della's parties,' Grizelda said. 'Like the one she had when we met. You know, I did think you were familiar, but I couldn't place you. That's one of the reasons why I kept hanging about the restaurant. That and watching over Ella because Mellie didn't and someone had to. I still can't believe that I didn't recognize you in the three years Ella lived under your roof!'

Grace shrugged. 'My twenty-five-year-old self looks as different from what I looked like two years ago as you look now compared to how you looked like ten minutes ago.'

'Eh, you got me there.' Grizelda smiled. 'By the way, how *did* you end up here?' Grizelda asked.

'I died.'

'Died? You look good for a dead girl.' The other woman smirked.

'I died in London while having Henry. Then I got an offer to become a guardian angel. But I had to relocate here with Peter and take in Ella and the twins. In exchange for getting to raise Henry for three years.'

'Why only three?' Grizelda looked puzzled.

Grace shrugged. 'I guess that's how long someone was willing to lend me their body.'

'You were using someone else's body?' The witch's eyes were as wide as saucers. 'Do tell.'

'Yes. I died from an aneurysm. And since this dimension is tricky and Time keeps switching around, then I never knew when I was going to keel over again. It was horrible knowing I could die while I was bathing Henry or going down the stairs with him. I didn't want to kill my child. So, the Agency of Guardian Angels arranged for me to borrow someone else's body for a few years. But made to look like I was when I had Henry - two stone heavier from all the fertility drugs I had been taking for ten years. That's why you didn't recognize me.'

Grizelda wolf-whistled. 'Where's yours then?'

'My what?'

'Your body.'

Grace smiled, but the smile didn't reach her eyes. 'This is me. I got my body back when Henry turned three. Except I went back on the deal and didn't take up serving as a guardian. I didn't want to abandon Henry. Or Peter. So...'

'So, they gave you back your own body with the aneurysm but cursed you to be a wolf?! That's unfair!'

Grace shrugged. 'I wouldn't say I was cursed. And the Agency doesn't think it is unfair. They think they are setting a cautionary example. On some level, it feels like payback, but I don't care anymore. I chose this. I can be a wolf. My son's pet wolf, if I have to. At least I get to be near him. And Peter.'

Grizelda digested this for a while. 'Well, aren't we a jolly pair.'

Grace smiled again.

'Whose body did you borrow? Anyone I know?' Grizelda asked absent-mindedly, biting down on a Madeleine small cake and passing Grace a bowl of freshly baked cookies that she had asked the table cloth to produce.

'Morgana's,' Grace said, taking the bowl.

'Morgana's?!?' Grizelda's jaw dropped and cookie crumbs fell out.

'Yes, Morgana's. Why are you horrified? I know she's a Fairy Queen and all, but...'

'Not just a Fairy Queen,' Grizelda said. 'She's the most feared Fairy Queen there is! Nobody messes with her flower colony. She has spies everywhere. Everyone begs her for favors. Spells. Curses. She is the most powerful witch of this dimension. A legend. And you're indebted to her now?' Grizelda asked. 'Poor lamb.'

Grace shook her head. 'No. Morgana owed a debt to Gabriel, the Boss of the Agency of Guardian Angels, and he called it in.'

'Wait, he did you a favor by calling in her debt? Must be some debt Morgana had.' Grizelda's eyes goggled. 'This guy Gabriel must have a serious case of hots for you.' Marina winked.

'He can't have the hots. He's an angel. They are neutral. And I prefer not to talk about it,' Grace said primly.

'Hey, I told you my deepest, darkest secrets. Spill.'

Grace chewed on her lip. 'I... I don't feel the same way about him. Not anymore. Not since I met Peter. And I have it on good authority that Gabriel orchestrated that meeting after Peter had lost the love of his life. So, Gabriel brought us together. His feelings, past or present, are moot.'

'Are you sure he knows this?' Grizelda asked.

Grace stayed silent. Pointing to the purple bottle, she asked, 'If you only need one dose to change and go back, why do you have a whole bottle?'

Grizelda sighed. 'Fate thought I would miss my old form and want to change back to it on occasion. I guess I'm less vain than she thought I would be. In my former life, I'm a singer in an all-girls pop band, I have a glitzy life, a hunk of a boyfriend and amazing friends...' Grizelda went quiet.

Grace looked at the bulbous vessel that contained her humanity. 'There's plenty now, but it will run out at some point, if you keep feeding it to me. Will you be able to make more?'

'Do I look like I know advanced potions and we're in Hogwarts?' Grizelda *huffed*. 'Temporary Goddess of Luck, not a proper witch, may I remind you.'

'Yes, but you may stumble on the recipe by mistake or...sheer Luck?' Grace winked at the old woman.

Grizelda *tap-tapped* her chin. 'Well, if you put it that way... I could try...to stumble.'

12. The Princess

Peter

Peter watched Henry sitting by the window, looking longingly at the woods. He probably wished he was out there, discovering the tricky paths with his wolf. Not yet. Not when a family dinner was due. Red tugged on his shirt collar, leaned his elbows onto the sill and scanned the ferns.

A horse neighed.

Clackety-clack. Clackety-clack.

The sounds appeared to be slowing and becoming louder.

Henry leaned out the window to see the road better.

'The princess is coming!' he told Peter and ran out the door as a carriage shaped like a giant golden pumpkin stopped in front of the huntsman's lodgings.

Peter stopped what he was doing and wiped his hands on a cloth.

The footman hopped down, yanked the stairs out and lay down a sturdy red carpet in between the carriage and the stairs to the house.

Only then did he open the carriage door, which was embossed with a crest sporting a lion standing by a sword sticking out of a stone.

'Daddy!' squealed a girl, who was decked out in the finest light-blue dress, as she flung herself into Peter's arms and all he could do was catch her.

A small boy of two peeked out from inside the carriage. 'Mama?' Seeing Henry standing a few feet away, the toddler smiled wide. 'Henly!'

'Hi, David!' Henry waved. 'Hi, Ella!'

'Come on out, pumpkin,' Ella said, taking her son by the hand and adjusting her caramel-brown ringlets with her other hand. 'You remember your grand-dad and auntie Greta?' Greta came out, wiping her hands on her apron.

David nodded and was helped down by the footman.

He ran into Henry's waiting arms and they disappeared into the innards of the house, leaving Peter to wonder how he had become a granddad at the tender age of forty.

'Try not to get him too dirty this time!' Ella yelled after the boys.

'What about Nick? Your husband didn't come then?' Peter asked.

'He prefers everyone but me calls him Nicholas or Prince Nicholas. He needs to have authority to be taken seriously when he takes the throne,' Ella rebuked him. 'I guess, he has been cautious about these get-togethers.'

Greta *huffed*. 'Avoiding them, you mean. Nicholas doesn't mind enjoying our dinners at The Duchess.'

Ella smiled. 'That's because at the restaurant he can be himself. Schmooze and cruise. With you lot, he's a bit lost. He knew whom he married. He just doesn't know how to act around...'

'Commoners is the word you're looking for,' Greta said.

Peter motioned for everyone to follow. 'Come on in, darling, before you catch cold in all that lace.'

Ella shrugged. 'I don't know if Nicholas thinks in these terms, given that Queen Belle used to be a village girl herself, but castle life changes people.'

'Yes, it distances them from the rest of us,' said Greta, looking pointedly at Ella who ignored her and went to stand by the window. 'Sit down, Your Highness,' Greta said as Ella ruffled her huge skirt. 'Or are you going to have your dinner standing?'

Ella frowned, not really looking at anybody. She seemed to be listening to the sounds of the forest and Peter perked up his ears as well.

13. Bored

At the hut

After dinner, Ella excused herself for some fresh air. To her surprise, Greta saw her sister go down the path and into the woods.

Half an hour later, the princess knocked on the witch's door.

'Hello, Granny,' Ella said, storing her eggshell-colored parasol in the corner. She pricked her finger and *tap-tapped* a glass eye on the door-frame. When it turned bright red, Ella sighed and mumbled, 'We'll keep trying.'

'Where'd you leave the carriage?' Grizelda asked. 'And the kid?'

'At Father's.'

The witch spun around. 'You walked here?'

Ella glared. 'I am perfectly capable of walking, thank you very much. It's not that everything is done for me, you know.'

'Isn't it then?'

Ella smiled a tight smile. 'Not that I want to be hands on. Belle does that and it looks tiring. But the whole being pretty in the corner thing gets old after a while.'

'Beauty has its advantages. If it goes together with brains.' The witch winked.

Ella laughed out loud. 'You know, despite my brown hair, no foreign dignitary has ever suspected me of having those.'

'That's because you have a nice pair of these.' The older woman motioned to her chest. 'Perhaps you should use all your assets to your advantage, girl?'

Ella laughed again and hugged the old woman. 'I love how you still treat me the same. Everyone I knew at school is just plain weird around me now. Bowing and scraping.'

'Don't tell me you're not enjoying some of it.'

Ella had to have a bit of a think. 'You know, as awful as some girls were to me at school – Betty Bonfleur in particular and the Cinders-Cinders moniker she tried to stick me with – I don't hold a grudge. It's difficult to hold a grudge when I'm happy.' Ella sighed.

'So why are you here?' Granny cocked her head. 'Tea?'

Ella nodded.

Grizelda went in search of something. 'So, what's got your knickers in a twist this time? Trouble in paradise already?' The witch cackled, busying herself, laying out a tattered table cloth. 'Whenever someone says they are happy could be they mean exactly the opposite.'

'Granny!' Ella rolled her eyes. 'Weren't you supposed to make tea? Why are you minding that tatty table cloth like it's the most precious thing you own?'

'Because it is,' Grizelda said. 'I'm glad this, too, came together with the hut or I'd have had to buy a kettle and pans and all of them cooking appliances from the Warriors, our mysterious manly procurers of all things bootleg.'

'How can a worn table cloth be helpful in preparing dinner? I hope you don't clean things with it.' Ella wrinkled her nose.

'Yes, yes, things are always prepared when you lot come around. But you took me by surprise today. Observe,' Grizelda said, waving at Ella to take a seat. '*Skatert samobranka, a nu ka nakroi-ka nam, serdeshnaja na stol, pozhaluista. A davai poprobujem Francuzskuju kuhnju sevodnja, a?*'

To Ella, she whispered, 'I asked the magic cloth for French cuisine.'

The table cloth flipped an edge and dishes started appearing one after another. Onion soup terrine with a ladle. Escargot. Mussels. Sweet and savoury crêpes. Éclairs. Salads. Chocolate soufflé. Several quiches. Coq au vin. Bouillabaisse. Cheeses. Wine. The works. When scarcely any room remained, Grizelda said 'Stop! *Spasibo bolshoe!*'

Ella picked up a creamy éclair and stuffed it in her mouth. 'Mmm....' She rolled her eyes and sighed. 'Heaven. Which is how it is with Nicholas and me at the palace, thank you very much.'

'Still waiting for why you're here,' Granny said, perusing a small appetizer with onion jam and slurping her tea.

'I wish I could do more,' Ella sighed wistfully. 'I've had princess lessons for three years now, with a bit of a reprieve when David was born. But except for delivering a lecture at my old school, I've not done anything useful. Oh, forget it. You wouldn't understand anyway.'

'Don't you pull that princess crap with me. Say what you want or don't say it at all.'

'I'm bored!' Ella blurted out and cupped her hand to her mouth.

'Finally, the truth. Spill it out, girl.'

Ella's nose colored pink. 'Mind you. I don't want to complain. I'm not... Everything is just perfect. Too perfect. My husband. My child. My life. And I'm bored out of my mind at the palace. I wish there was something interesting to do!'

'Everyone and their wishes,' Granny mumbled. 'Careful what you wish for, you just might get it, girl. What are you missing? Excitement? Adventure? Intrigue?'

Ella nodded. 'Yes to all of the above! You know, the older DeVille, the baron?' When Granny looked blank, Ella gave her The Look. 'John's father? The reason for me trying to enlist your services a few years ago, before I knew we were related.'

'Ah, that John.' The witch smirked. 'You didn't try. You did enlist my services. I zapped him good.'

'And thank you for that! But you didn't zap his dad,' Ella said. 'Which is why that old lech tried to blackmail me before he disappeared,' Ella said, looking haughty, fingering the lace on her sleeve.

'And?'

'I laughed in his face and told him Nick knows everything about my life before we met.'

'And?'

'And then I went and told Nick about everything about my life before we met. Including about John taking advantage of me and me getting pregnant and even about John palming me off to his dad. I even told Nick how, for a moment, I doubted whether to have David... but that matters fell into perspective when I realized the baby would be the only thing left of Nick that I would be able keep when on the run.'

'Good girl.' The witch nodded, looking pensive. 'I refused to give you the herbs to get rid of a royal baby, but I like that you managed to be honest with your husband.'

The pink reached Ella's cheeks. 'Thank you! If you're wondering whether the baron's and John's disappearance had anything to do with me, I did ask and Nick said he didn't do anything terrible to them. Just gave Evelyn DeVille – the lech's former wife – directions to where she could find the baron. None of them were ever heard of again. I presume Evelyn got her revenge.'

'Well, if it's intrigue you crave,' the witch winked, 'find it.' Seeing Ella perk up, Granny decided to issue a warning. 'I'm not saying you should go create it yourself. Never create trouble for yourself, if you can avoid it. Other people will do that plenty. But if you can suss out trouble – with your gifts especially – then perhaps you should?'

Ella licked her fingers. 'My gifts... Now there's a thought. But that means I would have to get upset with someone so I can form an emotional bond to be able to listen in on their thoughts.'

'Then perhaps you should practice getting upset at people? Or – just a suggestion –practice reaching out to the other person's thoughts and see if they open up to you without you going off kilter?'

Kind of like this?

This is easy. I'm your Granny. You've grown to love me since all the lies were cleared up. And I've always loved you. Love is a stronger emotional bond than hate.

Out loud Granny asked, 'What's your range, sugar?'

Ella twitched one shoulder. 'At the black and white ball, when Nicholas and I "met for the first time", I could hear Grace all the way from the castle, which is what... two miles from our old home?'

Granny tapped her chin. 'Let me see... Your father's house is three miles away, is it not? Can you hear him?'

Ella's eyebrows shifted together and as she shut her eyes, she gripped her head with her hands. 'Give me a second. I think I can hear someone...' She shook her head. 'Nope, it's gone.'

'Well, two miles is good, too,' Granny said.

Ella looked thoughtful. 'Have you heard... seen... unusual things... people... in the forest? Maybe someone hiding who shouldn't... be here?' Ella asked.

'Why?'

'You're going to think I'm bonkers, but I thought I sensed someone. Just now, when I visited Father. Someone who isn't around anymore. I tried searching for her on the walk here, but I didn't hear a peep.'

'What do you mean?' Granny narrowed her eyes at her granddaughter.

Ella closed her eyes. 'Hang on, someone *is* out there. In the woods.'

'I don't think I have any visitors coming today. Let me see.' Granny reached for her mirror.

Ella's eyes flew wide open. 'Wait... I can hear HER. But... but... That can't be!'

'Who did you hear, dear?' Granny asked.

'I have to speak to Father,' Ella said and ran out the door, nearly losing one of her shoes on the wooden stairs.

14. Beyond All Recognition

Peter

The huntsman was teaching his two-year old grandson how to draw a toy bow when Ella burst in, her muddy skirts aflounder and her face flushed from the sprint. Gone was the cool princess who was afraid to sit down for fear of smudging her dress.

Peter rose. 'What's the matter, darling? Is someone after you? Is Granny alright?'

Ella shook her head and kept panting. She leaned on the door jamb, doubled over and raised her hand. 'Gimme. A. Minute.'

Peter got up and reached for a jug of water on the windowsill, with David trailing him, pressed against his leg. He poured Ella a glass of water as David continued to stare at his Mama with concern.

Ella gulped the water down and sagged onto the closest chair. 'I need to talk to you.'

The huntsman put David in a chair next to his mother and nudged paper and crayons his way. 'Do you want to color the rainbow, David?' When the kid began to color over the lines with his tongue sticking out, Peter gave Ella a curt nod. 'Tell me.'

'You'll consider me crazy, but I think I... I heard Grace,' Ella said, stroking David's hair. 'Believe me, I'd know my stepmother's judgmental voice anywhere. Ever since I hated her for a second – well, I did and had good reason to – I could hear her thoughts. But now... How can that be possible? She left the kingdom, she left you and Henry, didn't she?' Ella fixed her eyes on her stepfather.

Peter shrugged. 'What's it to you?'

'What's it to me? You're my Father!'

Peter raised an eyebrow at her.

'Well, you are the only one I've ever known. You're as good as. And you care about her, so I care about her. Besides, you know how she helped me.'

Peter looked straight ahead. 'Be that as it may. I don't know.'

'You don't know what?' Ella narrowed her eyes.

'I don't know if it is her.'

Ella's jaw dropped. 'But why? Don't you know what your wife looks like? Or are you saying she has changed?'

Peter smiled a wry smile. 'Beyond all recognition.'

Ella *ah*-ed. 'She was disfigured?!? How? What happened?' she breathed out in one go.

'You would think so. She took to the woods where she still is.'

'And you let her live in the woods by herself?!? Disfigured and alone?'

'She's ill equipped to live with people now.'

Ella looked aghast. 'Well, of course she would be, if she's disfigured!'

Peter shook his head. 'I never said she was disfigured. Actually, she's...she's magnificent! She's just...not human.'

'Not human? What, has she turned into a tree or an animal or something?'

Peter exacted a few slow nods.

Ella looked around the hut and zeroed in on the rifle mounted on the wall.

'You became a huntsman and moved the family to the woods straight after Grace disappeared.'

Peter kept silent.

'That was because of her, wasn't it?' Ella asked.

Peter nodded.

'I thought you had lost it. That you had to escape from grief or shame over your wife mistreating your daughter and then leaving you. You said you were grieving! Gods, I even thought for a second you killed her and buried her in the woods!'

Both of Peter's eyebrows shot up.

'And this whole time, for the past two years, you have not been hunting animals, but keeping an eye on her?' The princess pointed to the woods.

'Oh, I've been hunting animals alright,' Peter said motioning to the rabbit skins hanging above the fireplace. 'But she needed protecting, so I stepped up.'

'Protecting? From whom?'

'The rest of us.'

'Papa, I'm home! Greta said it will be a slow night and that she would be alright by herself at The Duchess!' Henry said coming in through the door, shaking pine needles from his red T-shirt. 'Oh, hi, again, Ella!'

Ella took in the red shirt and asked, 'You let Henry wander around by himself with the wolves on the loose? He's five!'

'That he is. But he's well looked after,' Peter said.

'By whom?'

Peter gave Ella The Look and shook his head.

'Gr... *She* looks after Henry?'

Peter didn't say anything.

'Are you talking about my wolf?'

Ella's jaw dropped for the second time. 'Your WOLF? *Your* wolf? Father?' Now it was Ella's turn to give Peter The Look.

'Yes, my wolf. She's watching over me,' Henry said.

Peter shook his head at Ella and put his finger to his lips.

Ella shot up from her seat and put her hands to her hips, looking more like a bargaining market maid than a princess. 'You two are serious?'

Peter and Henry looked at each other and shrugged at Ella in unison.

'Henry, why don't you go outside and see where Hans is. I know he loves the forest, but it's supper-time and he hasn't even seen Ella today. Go fetch him, please.'

The boy nodded.

Ella opened her mouth to say something when Peter shook his head again.

The huntsman handed his son a lantern. 'Go that way,' he said and pointed the boy in the direction of the echoing *thwacks*.

When the little boy was out of earshot, Ella demanded, 'Why is Gr...*she* a wolf? And why doesn't Henry know about it? Why doesn't anybody know about it?'

'Would you tell your son that his father was a fearful beast, if say Nicholas left one day and could never come back?'

Ella's mouth formed an O. 'But why is she a wolf? Could she always shift into a wolf? Was she bitten? Do we have werewolves roaming the kingdom now?'

The huntsman shook his head. 'Hold your horses. There aren't werewolves in the kingdom. That I know of. Grace was not bitten nor was she a shifter to start with. She chose this punishment for not wanting to honor her agreement to become a guardian angel.'

Ella sat back down again. 'Guardian angel. Grace had agreed to become a guardian angel and then changed her mind?'

Peter nodded. 'Yes.'

Ella wiped her brow and mumbled, 'I remember meeting one. That should have tipped me right off.'

'What was that?' Peter asked.

'Nothing. Was that in exchange for arranging my happily ever after, by any chance, do you know?'

Peter hemmed and hawed. 'Yes and no. Your happily ever after was just half of the bargain. The other half was borrowing someone else's body for three years.'

Ella looked at him like he was insane. 'She borrowed a body?'

Peter didn't even blink.

'For the entire three years that I knew her, she was someone else?' Ella paled. 'That would explain a lot...'

'Grace was herself in spirit, but in someone else's body which was fashioned to look like her. Physically,' Peter said.

Seeing Ella looking puzzled, Peter tried to explain. 'It's complicated. She looked like herself, but it was hard for me to forget she really wasn't. And sometimes she didn't act like herself.'

Ella had a flashback to the evening when Grace had almost slapped Henry. 'Yeah... Wait... So, I never knew the real Grace? The whole three years?' The young woman looked sad. 'Someone else's body helped me get ready for my wedding? Someone else's body hugged me when I had the crappiest day of my life? Someone else was awful to me?'

'Oh no, that was all her. She made a deal to be awful to you.'

'She what?'

Peter shrugged. 'She agreed to be the necessary evil in your life to help you get your happily ever after.'

'In exchange for what? Her happily ever after?' Ella scoffed.

Peter was slow to respond. 'Yes. Otherwise, she would have been dead and I would have had to raise Henry alone far, far away from here. She died giving birth to him. Before that, even, to be honest. Grace was given a second chance to keep the family together, but we had to relocate here. And take in you and the twins.'

Ella stayed silent, processing it all. 'Mellie would have sufficed as the necessary evil. Grace was kind to me. In the end. Grace made good on her promise. Why did the angels punish her?'

'Part of the deal was that she would become a guardian herself when Henry turned three. She refused.'

'So, they turned her into a wolf?' Ella looked horrified.

Peter nodded. 'If she didn't want to be a good example, she was going to be a horrible warning.'

'But that's unfair!'

'Given the chance, I'm sure she'd do the same all over again,' Peter said.

'Ella! Long time, no see. How are you, sis?' Bellowed a young man with a mop of flaming hair, who made Peter look like a dwarf, ducking to get through the door- way. Seeing the princess blanch, he crooked a toothy smile and kept walking toward her with outstretched arms.

'Hans! Don't you dare...' Ella started saying when she caught sight of herself in the mirror. 'Oh, gods. I look manky. Ah, very well, I could use a grimy hug,' she mumbled into her younger brother's shoulder.

'As if you could have stopped me doing that.' Hans laughed.

She slapped him on the arm. 'You've grown a lot since I last saw you, little brother. Except you're not so little anymore. You're only fifteen, but going on twenty! What do they feed you? Or should I ask what do Greta and Granny keep feeding you at The Duchess?' Ella's playfulness evaporated.

'What's the matter, sis?' Hans asked. 'Haven't you eaten anything yet?'

'Food isn't the problem,' Ella bit off.

'Why the sour face then?' Hans asked.

Ella rolled her eyes and thought that now was as good time as any to extract herself from her stepfather's house. 'Oh, my. I have to go back to Granny's again. I left my parasol there, silly me.'

'Take the carriage this time,' Peter suggested as he started collecting David's toys.

'Of course.' Ella took one look at her muddy dress and sighed. 'This dress is ruined. I might as well change at Granny's. It's more private there. Luckily, I always have a spare dress with me when we leave the palace in case... in case...'

'In case your grimy relatives hug you.' Hans snorted.

'No, in case David gets his tiny little hands dirty and I can't help cuddling him.' Ella smiled. 'But yes, it helps against your ministrations as well, brother dearest.'

15. The Curse

At the hut

Ella's parasol kept falling across the threshold. Either it was the parasol or the hut fidgeting, but Granny finally gave up, mumbled, something about 'bad omens' and went looking for a place to hang the damn thing.

'Why was Ella here?'

Grizelda spun around toward her kitchen and the back entrance of her hut to find a petite woman in a purple cloak standing there.

'Hello to you, too, Your Majesty,' Grizelda said, casting a glance at her bedroom where Grace was changing after coming in from the woods.

'Don't you hello me. Why was she here?' Queen Belle demanded, drawing back her hood to reveal dark-brown hair, plaited to the side in a French braid. She threw her gloves onto the table and fixed her brown eyes on the witch.

'You're afraid she wants to keep her vainglorious body slim and has come to get rid of a baby? Don't you fret,' Grizelda said, in a louder voice than usual.

'I'm not worried about that anymore.' Belle waved her off, her rings glinting in the light of the single candle on the witch's long table. 'We already have David.'

The witch raised an eyebrow. 'So, you don't care if she gets rid of a potential prince or princess?'

'That light should not turn blue for a good fifteen years if not more,' Belle said, taking the few steps required to get to the front door to tap the little glass eye, which promptly showed her a red light. She looked startled. 'But I didn't even prick myself! How...?' She tapped the contraption again. 'Well, at least it's working.'

'Yes, you're not up the duff. Why is that? The Beast doesn't want you no more?' The old woman cackled.

'Crude. And none of your business, witch,' the queen said.

'I prefer Granny these days,' the witch said.

As Belle turned to inspect her contraption once more Grizelda saw Grace poke her head out from her bedroom and motioned for her to hide.

Belle turned back to face her and raised an eyebrow at Grizelda's hand motions.

'Fruit flies,' Grizelda said.

'So, are you going to tell me why Ella was here or not?' Belle asked.

'Not before you tell me why that light won't turn blue for fifteen years,' the witch said. 'I'm pretty sure I will need to know now, since I will need to train up an apprentice, seeing that I'm not going to be around then.'

'Oh, don't be tiresome. Of course, you'll be around. You're too young to die. Witches live long lives, don't they?' Belle looked uncertain. 'Unless this is your way of telling me that you're dying.'

'We all die at some point. Sometimes even unexpectedly. Why not tell me now?' Grizelda parried, thinking about how she was going to get Grace out of here. Grace would turn back in an hour and could jump out of the window, but meanwhile, she was stuck in the bed- room, eavesdropping. Then again, if she herself hadn't recognized Grace, maybe Belle wouldn't either. 'In fact, you should tell me now, while I have my apprentice here.'

'You do?' Belle gasped and then caught herself. 'You do? Why didn't you tell me? Where is she?'

Grizelda prayed Grace would play along and hollered, 'Greta, come on out!'

A few long seconds passed. Then the bedroom door creaked open. Grace appeared in the doorway and curtseyed, avoiding Belle's gaze.

'This is not Greta. Or if it is, she has magically aged ten years since last I saw her at The Duchess yesterday,' Belle remarked, looking the newcomer up and down.

'Plenty of people are called Greta. She happens to be one of those people.' Grizelda shrugged.

'Why doesn't she speak for herself? Is she mute?'

'Your Majesty,' Grace rasped and did another curtsy.

'What's wrong with her voice?' Belle asked.

'She doesn't talk much. An admirable quality in an apprentice and a witch, don't you think?' Grizelda winked in conspiratorial fashion. 'I know I couldn't stand someone jabbering at me day and night and you can rest assured your secrets are safe here, be it me or my apprentice who keeps them.'

Belle thought about it and nodded curtly. 'Very well. If you are that worried about your longevity as to take on an apprentice, then I guess I do need to tell you the whole truth about that contraption,' Belle pointed at the front door frame, 'and why when it turns blue, it is paramount that the baby should be carried to term.'

Grizelda mumbled something about nobody ever telling the whole truth, but quieted when Belle frowned.

'I also need to tell Ella,' Belle said, 'but since you are the vanguard of protecting royal babies, I might as well tell you now.'

'If this is gonna be a long talk, take a seat, Your Majesty.' The witch motioned to the only comfortable chair in the room, perched herself on the edge of the long bench and motioned for Grace to do so as well.

Belle rolled her eyes and mumbled something about 'No standing on ceremony between relatives'.

'As you very well know, blue light means it's a royal baby,' Belle said, taking a seat on the edge of the armchair, keeping her back straight. 'The only royal baby Nicholas will ever have. That's why I told you I'd have you hung, drawn and quartered if you dared to abort it.'

Grizelda nodded. 'Yes, thank you, I remember the blue light. You had that bloodsucking contraption installed in my door when Nick turned fifteen.'

'Nicholas, if you don't mind,' Belle said as Grace mouthed, 'Bloodsucking?'

'The thing requires a few drops of the girl's blood and if it turns green, it's a normal baby and if it turns blue, it's a royal baby.'

'And if it turns red, there is no baby,' Grizelda finished.

'Why fifteen?' Grace asked.

'Age has nothing to do with it. I had this thing delivered from the Warriors and installed here where young girls come with their troubles when I found a girl sneaking out of Nicholas' quarters. For three years, I thought that I had missed it. That one of the first few girls he had been with had got rid of the baby when she got in the family way. Or that a girl had hid herself away to have my son's only child in secret. So, I had all of these girls found out and tracked down to see if any of them had had children. No such luck. So, I thought I had been late with my precautions, but I had hope... I also regretted that I didn't have it installed as soon as Nicholas was born.'

'That would have been overkill,' Grizelda said.

'Imagine my surprise when I was alerted that the light had turned blue. Now this, this is a state secret and I could have you...'

'Hung, drawn and quartered, got it,' Grace said.

'If you dare speak of it to anyone, you will be,' Belle assured her. 'The child was Ella's. She came here before Nicholas officially rescued her from her wicked stepmother.'

Grace tried not to smile.

'Why are you smiling? And why do you look rather familiar?' Belle narrowed her eyes at the witch's apprentice.

'Why is Nicholas the only child?' Grace asked instead, wiping the smile off her face.

'Yes, well noted, apprentice!' Grizelda positioned herself so that she was between Grace and the queen. 'Your Majesty, why do you think Nick...Nicholas and Ella will have only one child? Surely, as Nicholas is young and Ella is willing, they will have more...'

'No.' Belle's shoulders sagged and she sat back into the chair, her rigid posture deflated. 'That's not how the curse operates.'

'The curse?' Grace echoed.

'Morgana's curse.'

'Well, doesn't she get everywhere.' Grizelda wolf-whistled. 'What'd she do this time?'

'This time? Wait, what else has she done in my kingdom?' Belle asked.

The witch laughed so hard she almost fell off the bench. 'Your...your...*your* kingdom? Muahhaahaa...'

Under Belle's haughty stare the laughter mutated into hiccoughs and Grizelda went to her kitchen in search of water. 'I'm sorry, I thought you knew it wasn't *yours* as such,' Grizelda said when she came back, carrying a teapot. 'I'm sure Your Majesty is aware that your kingdom is not the only one. There are also the Warriors and there used to be Dragons.'

'The Warriors are just a small compound up North and nobody has seen a dragon in these parts for years. They are not separate kingdoms,' Belle argued as Grace perked up her ears.

'Yes, but they used to be separate kingdoms within what is now known as the Magic Kingdom, even though the Warriors have no official king, but a chief and nobody truly knows about the dragons as we haven't seen a single one in years. This Kingdom is for the people that live here and for you to serve them as well as you can as a ruler, not for you to pretend you are the be all and end all. Which you are not.' Grizelda tapped the teapot. 'Tea?'

Belle cocked her head. 'How very interesting. You know, that is something Tom, King Thomas whom you all lovingly call the Beast behind his back used to say. A long time ago. When we had just met... for the second time.'

'Do tell.' The witch's eyes sparkled as she started pouring tea onto the tablecloth. Before the first drop hit the table a cup appeared underneath the spout.

'Some other time.' Belle smoothed her skirts and inclined her head, accepting a tea cup from the older woman.

'At least tell me about the curse. Maybe you misunderstood?' Grizelda pried.

Belle shook her head. 'There was no misunderstanding when Thomas turned human at midday the day after I returned. He was quite surprised, having been a beast for two years straight. He couldn't stop walking on all fours for an hour. That's when I knew Morgana's curse had set in.'

'You mean the curse you cast had started working,' Granny's "apprentice" interjected.

'I might have cast it, but Morgana came up with it. Her curse cancelled out the permanence spell Thomas and his fairy godmother had concocted,' Belle said and Grace frowned, casting a glance at the vial with the potion.

'When a year later Nicholas was born in the early hours of the morning, there was no mistaking that a man, not a beast walked into our bedchamber to see his newborn. After we had Nick, Tom could turn any time he liked. I knew it had to be Morgana's counter-curse when despite all the efforts, Nicholas was the only child we ever managed to have. That's when I knew I had to make sure my son's only child would survive, no matter who the mother was,' Belle said and sighed, not noticing that color had drained from "Greta's" face.

Grizelda whispered something and the ratty table cloth filled itself with dishes of sweets. 'Let me get this straight. You asked Morgana, the fiercest Fairy Queen of them all to lift Beast's curse, so he...'

'..and his whole castle...' Belle chimed in.

'...and his whole castle could become human again in exchange for what?'

'My firstborn and his firstborn and so on,' Belle's voice trailed off, 'becoming beasts.'

'So, when a child is born, the curse is passed on? You let her tie the curse to your whole bloodline?' the witch asked.

Belle nodded curtly, biting her lips. 'I told Morgana I'd give her anything if she made Thomas human again. But I forgot to add "permanently human" and I forgot to agree it could only be something that I could do or give and never someone else,' Belle whispered.

'So, she cursed his whole bloodline?' the apprentice asked, her lips in a thin line.

'My bloodline. Which also means Tom's bloodline since we have Nicholas. Did you know Morgana engineered Tom's curse in the first place and manipulated someone else to cast it?' Belle said. 'The one she gave me to "free" him was a curse upon a curse.'

Grizelda wolf-whistled again. 'That Morgana, she's pulling a lot of strings in a lot of fairytales. It's like she wants to play Fate.' The witch narrowed her eyes. 'You do know she was behind Ella and Nick getting it on...erm... hitting it off?'

Belle gritted her teeth. 'Why am I even surprised.'

'Are you upset?' Grace asked.

Belle shrugged. 'No. Ella's been good for Nicholas. Of course, we had to ease her into the family secret when she became too suspicious, finding Nicholas gone from their bed after midnight and sleeping in until midday. When we told her, she handled seeing her husband turn into a lion rather well. And then David was born and Nicholas' beastly episodes ended. Now he can turn at will.'

'But if the curse was passed on when Ella's son was born...' Grace said, looking pained. She wiped a few beads of sweat form her forehead and having caught Grizelda's eye motioned toward the bedroom.

'Yes, now, Nicholas can turn into a Beast when he wants to. As can Tom,' Belle said, 'but the curse will hit David on his eighteenth birthday.'

'Greta, you go lie down,' Grizelda said. 'You were up all night, erm...brewing potions, so you deserve a little kip. I think you have heard the essentials about this particular customer. The lesson is over for today.'

Grace scurried off to the bedroom.

'Where were we? Ah yes, each time a new kid is born down the line, the father acquires the ability to shape-shift when he wants, not when he has to?' Grizelda asked.

'Yes,' Belle said.

'Does Ella know her kid is cursed and what awaits David on his eighteenth?' Grizelda asked.

'Not yet, but she will. Someday I'll have to tell her about the importance of that thingamajig on your door.' Belle waved at Grizelda's front door.

'Consider you just did,' Ella said, stepping inside, wearing a plain brown dress.

'How much did you hear?' Belle asked.

'Plenty.'

'Well then,' Grizelda said and motioned for her granddaughter to sit, but Ella shook her head.

'I'm not staying. David fell asleep in the carriage.' The young woman zeroed in on her mother-in-law. 'When were you going to tell me? When David reaches puberty? Do I have to come here with a few drops of his blood to reset that contraption?' Ella pointed at the glass eye.

Belle shook her head. 'This contraption, as you say, was set to my blood. It's my bloodline I exchanged for Tom not being a Beast forever.'

'Yes, but David is not just some abstract bloodline. He is flesh and blood. My flesh and my blood, not just yours. How could you?'

'I'm sorry, Ella. I was young and naive. I didn't know Morgana would twist my offer to forever. Or that someone else would pay the price...'

'Still, how could you?'

Belle looked at her levelly. 'Let me tell you a story...'

Grizelda rolled her eyes and Ella crossed her arms.

Belle took a refilled cup from Grizelda and sat up straight. 'I met Thomas in the woods and didn't know at the time that he was the crown prince. Not that it would have mattered. We were sixteen. After my chores were done in the morning, I was free to roam the woods or read books. When I lent my cloak to a naked stranger left for dead by robbers, I never thought he would seek me out to return that item of clothing in person. Or that the stranger I had helped would turn out to be our future king. Thomas and I were just friends for almost a year. I didn't know he was royalty. Until the ball in the honor of his sixteenth birthday.'

Ella perked up. 'There was a ball?'

Belle nodded and her eyes misted over. 'There was a ball.'

16. Mishaps

When Belle finished telling Grizelda and Ella about how Beast had confided in her about his curse, she looked at Ella and said, 'Thomas told me Morgana had come up with his original curse. I thought she who made it would surely have a remedy against it.'

'You mean the counter-curse,' Ella pointed out.

'I served Morgana for a long time to earn the remedy. I didn't know it would be another curse,' Belle said. 'I was trying to help.'

'I'm trying not to judge, but you're making it very hard. A curse is never helpful, don't you know that?' Ella asked.

Belle cast her eyes down and swallowed. 'I didn't know that Tom and his fairy godmother had found an alternative solution. Thomas only told me there might have been another option when he turned human the day after I came back. By which time I had already cast my counter-curse.'

'You cast your curse *before* you got back?' Ella looked aghast. 'You cast a curse on your future husband without even asking him?!?'

Belle nodded and a tear trickled down her cheek. The queen looked wretched. 'I wanted it to be a nice surprise.'

'What was the other solution?' Ella asked through thin lips.

'Somehow, Tom and his fairy godmother Caroline had managed to make the spell permanent and tie it to the life of a magic rose. The spell was supposed to last for about six years. Although how, I cannot fathom. The flower had barely any petals left two years down the line. Where was I?'

'The spell,' Granny said from the shadows.

Belle sighed and continued. 'Caroline's permanent spell had made Tom a Beast full-time. She was dying and desperate and they didn't know what would happen after she was gone and no longer able to administer his curse every day. That curse might have turned permanent anyway upon her death. Thomas didn't know his godmother's spell would actually work. They didn't know how long the rose would really last. It was a made-up fairy spell, a fervent prayer of two desperate souls against the curse of a Fairy Queen. They didn't modify the part where the curse is broken if a girl falls in love with him and he with her and they seal the deal with a True Love's Kiss.'

'A True Love's Kiss would break any curse,' Ella muttered.

'Thomas and his godmother made it so that the kiss needed to happen before all the petals fell off,' Belle continued as if she hadn't heard her daughter-in-law.

'You were both already in love. So, you could have kissed and it could have worked without your interference?' Ella looked horrified.

'I tried! The kiss didn't work! All it did was jumpstart Morgana's curse, which undid Beast being Beast around the clock.'

'But you cursed his whole progeny!' Ella wailed. 'You, not Morgana!'

'None of us knew anything! We're not witches or fairies. I just wanted to help the man I loved!' Belle argued.

Grizelda mumbled something about a road to hell and good intentions.

'If you hadn't done what you did, the curse could have ended with Thomas!' Ella yelled.

'Tom would have been a Beast forever! We wouldn't have had Nicholas and you wouldn't have had David!' Belle yelled back.

'We will never know now, will we? Because you made things worse. The King's original curse now extends to all of his descendants!' Ella hissed. 'All of them!' She inhaled and closed her eyes. 'So, not only will David get a lovely coming-of-age present, getting to be hairy at night until he procreates, but all my other children will as well. Thanks!'

'Only David,' Belle whispered, white as a sheet.

'What do you mean only David? Only the firstborn is affected? So, if I have any daughters, they won't be hairy from midnight to midday?' Ella perked up.

'You can't have any daughters. David is all you get. I'm so sorry...' Belle whispered.

'What?!' Ella clenched her fists.

'The curse shifts from father to son. To limit the damage...' Belle said. 'Morgana said it would be easier to contain...'

'Morgana said? Morgana said?!?' The whites of Ella's eyes were showing. 'I can't believe how selfish you were! Why didn't you at least wait until you saw Thomas again and asked him if he wanted this? I know Thomas, he would have said no. He would never have wished any of this on his only child...or grandchild! You could have at least waited! ALL YOU HAD TO DO WAS COME BACK, FALL IN LOVE AND THEN KISS HIM!' Ella shouted at the top of her lungs, advancing on her mother-in-law, looking like she wanted to punch her.

Belle stood her ground. 'You don't understand! When we met again, he didn't even remember me! He tried to eat me! I didn't know he had been a Beast for two years. I thought he still changed only from midnight to midday. I didn't know the last time he had been human was when I left two years before! I was going back thinking his human half would remember he liked me. Maybe even a bit more than liked me. I didn't realize that the animal had taken over until I saw him again. I DID kiss him, but it wasn't a True Love's Kiss because HE DIDN'T LOVE ME ANYMORE!' Belle sagged against the chair. 'He had completely forgotten me. It was as if he never even knew me. As if we were never friends. As if he never had any feelings for me at all,' Belle whispered.

Ella shook her head, looking like a mutinous mule. 'I don't believe you. You've lied to your son. You've lied to me. I can't have any more children and David will turn into a...what exactly?'

'A lion, like Tom and Nick. On his eighteenth birthday,' Belle supplied. 'And you and Nick will have to be the ones who will have to instruct him through it. Have the celebration ball the night before, like I did for Nicholas.'

'I can't believe what you've done! Thomas' way could have worked!' Ella *huffed*.

'If you don't believe me that it was the only way, ask Thomas.' Belle stood up and headed for the front door, looking resigned. 'When I arrived, the rose had only very few petals left. It didn't last six years, like Tom hoped. The flower lasted six more months after I came back. Ask him and you'll see there was no other way.'

'Oh, I will,' Ella said, following her mother-in-law out.

Grizelda stood watch and saw Ella convincing Belle to tie her horse to the back of the carriage and they both climbed into the vehicle. She watched the carriage dwarf and disappear into the forest before she went to see if Grace was still in the house.

Ella

LATER THAT NIGHT, ELLA was feeling out of sorts after her spat with Belle at Granny's and was pacing the lush carpet in front of their four-poster bed. She had just finished telling Nicholas what Belle had told her. 'Why don't you ask your father, Nick how things really happened?' Ella suggested. 'We need to know if Belle is telling the truth.'

'Me go ask my kingly father to tell me the truth?' Nick asked and sat down on the broad window-sill.

In the moonlight, with his dark looks and chiseled features, her prince still looked every bit as dashing and Charming.

'We haven't had that sentiment here since... forever.'

'You mean honesty?' Ella smirked and sat next to him.

Nick tucked a stranded caramel-brown lock behind her ear. 'Yes, darling, that's why I thought you were such a fresh breath of air.'

'Well, apart from lying to me for the first eight months of our marriage about where you really spent your nights, you've always told me the truth. Why do you expect anything less from your parents?' Ella asked.

'Because they are my parents. Sometimes I think they have a million things they are not telling me. Like why was I ever the only child?'

Ella's smile faltered.

'Mother trusted me enough to tell me about the curse after I turned eighteen, but for instance, she never considered telling me it was Grace who invented the clever gadgets that she sold as her own.' Nick pushed off the window-sill, but Ella caught him by his sleeve.

'Separate issues, Nick. It's not that she didn't trust you. She had a difficulty telling you. But she had to tell you on the morning of your eighteenth birthday, because you were about to turn into a Beast come midnight, just like your father before you,' Ella said and traced the outline of his chest right where his shirt was unbuttoned.

'Yes, isn't it lucky that Maman did organize that masked ball and I met you the night before my eighteenth?' Nick winked and pulled his wife close.

'Somehow, I don't think luck had anything to do with it,' Ella said.

'Perhaps, but she never planned on you,' Nick whispered, making Ella color to her roots. 'Come on, you're still embarrassed by what brought us together?' His blue eyes searched her face.

'Grace's spiked chocolate cake and a bottle of wine,' Ella mumbled, feeling her cheeks with the back of her hand.

'I think it was the wine,' Nick said.

'I have it on good authority it was the spiked cake that had us acting all amorous.' Ella smacked his arm. 'And yes, I'm allowed to feel embarrassed about getting pregnant the first time I laid my eyes on you.'

'I think a bit more effort went into making David than just eye-gazing, my love.' Nick kissed Ella's neck, making her blush deepen. 'Would you like me to show you? Again?'

Ella let her husband's kisses stray all the way down to her elbow before she said, 'Not until you promise me that you'll speak to Tom and get to the bottom of this.'

'Anything you want,' Nick said, continuing his descent.

17. Back From the Dead

At the hut

After her visitors had gone, Grizelda was airing the rooms to clear the bad juju when Peter walked in and flopped a couple of dead rabbits onto the table.

'What, pray tell, do you want me to do with those?' she asked.

'Cook them. Give me half. Or don't. They're yours.'

'Oh, honey, I haven't cooked in decades and I don't intend to start now. Take them back. Put them over there!' She motioned toward her front door. 'Off the table, off! I'm sure you and your family will enjoy the stew more than I would. Tea?'

'I just wanted to say thank you,' Peter said.

'For what?'

'Thank you for looking after Henry. You know Grace would appreciate you reading him her fairytales. I can't bring myself to read them. When I see her handwriting, I keep hearing her voice and I just can't...'

'I know she appreciates it.'

The huntsman nodded.

'She told me,' Granny said.

'Told you?' Peter froze. 'What do you mean? She told you before...that she would appreciate it if you did this?'

'That, too. But she told me herself just recently.'

'How? Do you.... Have you seen her? Can you speak to wolves?'

'Of course.' Grizelda nodded. 'In fact, she was just here.'

Peter felt his legs falter and he sagged onto the bench.

Grizelda perked up. 'I think I hear the clackety clack of her claws. She's back!'

The bedroom door creaked and a familiar black snout peeked out.

Two bright green eyes flashed in the darkness beyond.

Peter froze. 'How did she get in?'

The snout retreated.

The witch went about making tea as if nothing out of the ordinary was going on.

'Trust the witch to let in a wolf,' the huntsman muttered.

Peter thought he imagined a purple glow coming from the bedroom.

There was a rustle and the door creaked again.

Peter looked up. A barefooted woman stepped out of the shadows, wearing a grey peasant dress that accentuated fewer curves than he remembered, sporting the same bright green eyes he'd recognize anywhere. She puffed back an errant curl.

Grace.

My Grace. In her human form.

Except she looked younger. Like she had when they had first met – stick thin, with her short black hair curling every which way and with question marks in her eyes. As if the last fifteen years had not happened.

'You're... You're...'

'Here,' she said and crossed the distance between them.

Peter stood up and reached for her wasp-thin waist.

'Hello, darling,' Grace said more throatily than he remembered. She put her hands on his chest and chuckled. 'Sorry, not used to talking.'

He shut his eyes and held her close as if she were made of glass, easing into her, exhaling the breath he didn't know he had been holding. 'It's you. It really is you. I've missed you,' he murmured into her hair, sitting down and drawing her into his lap in one swift motion.

Grace rubbed her cheek against his stubble and nestled closer in his arms. 'I've missed you, too.'

He nuzzled her neck, inhaling.

'Enough of the missing, more of the talking,' the witch intervened. 'Tea?'

Peter

TEN MINUTES LATER, Peter felt the familiar anger bubble up again.

How long has she been able to turn human? Why didn't she tell me?

'You used to be a wolf. All of the time. What changed?' Peter asked, looking cross.

Grace nodded. 'It's been two years. Forgot what it was like to be human. To have a shower.' Grace sniffed her hair and cringed. 'To talk.'

'Did you do this somehow, Grizelda?' Peter asked. 'Transform her back into a human being?'

Grizelda waved at Grace. 'This is temporary. Only the person who cast the curse can undo it.'

'How long have you been able to turn back?' Peter asked his wife with an unhealthy glint in his eye and unseated her from his lap.

'Just a few weeks. Granny...Grizelda didn't even think that the potion meant for her would work on me. She tried it on an off chance...' Grace said with effort, her voice low and raspy.

'A few weeks.' The huntsman stood up, running his hand through his hair.

'Yes, a few weeks ago, she fed me some potion with bread and I turned back!'

'Why didn't you tell me?' Peter asked, biting his lips.

'Now, hang on,' the witch jumped in.

'You've been turning back into a human for a few weeks already and you didn't think to seek me out?' Peter asked, his eyes darkening.

'I tried,' Grace sighed. 'The potion wears off in less than an hour. I tried getting to you. By the time I got to your home I was a wolf again. The potion is not meant...was never meant for me. It's hers.' Grace pointed at Granny.

'So, it's just my blind luck that I happened to pass by at the most opportune moment to find you here in human form?' Peter asked, gritting his teeth.

He got enthusiastic nods from both of the women.

'Why couldn't you have written me a note in that one hour and asked Grizelda to deliver it?'

Grizelda scratched her head. 'Now why didn't I think of that?'

Grace just looked surprised.

'I swear, living without smartphones in this dimension has addled my brain as to what elementary communication looks like,' the witch tried to joke.

The silence stretched half into tomorrow as Peter and Grace stared at each other.

'I never left the rooftop,' Peter told Grace.

'What?'

'I never left. Gabriel was so engrossed in punishing you, he didn't notice that I was still there. I saw you turn. Why do you think I moved into the woods and became the huntsman?'

'Because right about the time Grace "disappeared" a stupid wolf went against the pack, killed two sheep, the whole village wanted revenge and the post was open?' Grizelda offered.

'Yes. And no. The post was open. The villagers wanted revenge. And I didn't want anyone killing my wife while they were at it. So, I stepped up,' Peter said, grinding his teeth.

'But you hate killing things. You couldn't even write Mellie's character assassination in one of your exposés,' Grace said, touching his face. 'Back when you were running the newspaper around here.'

'The traps kill the rabbits. I just have to skin them.' Peter motioned at the bundle next to the door.

Grace stroked his shoulders. 'I thought I smelled blood.'

Peter closed his eyes and felt Grace wrap her arms around him from behind. 'We miss you, you know. All of us. I... We all grieved. For the public at large, you were missing, presumed dead,' Peter said. 'I moved the whole family to the woods so I could be near you. I took up being a huntsman, so I could protect the wolves and you from being lynched by the villagers for all manner of wrong, real and imagined.' Peter opened his eyes. 'When I did spot you, I wanted to...to stroke you, to comfort you, to touch you, goddamit! And I knew I couldn't because my human scent would drive the pack away.'

'Worse, your scent would have made the pack abandon the pups,' Grace muttered into his back.

Peter kept looking right in front of him. 'For the past two years I didn't know if there was anything human left of you in that wolf. And then you tell me that you have been able to turn human for weeks and you didn't tell me!' He clenched his fists.

'I'm sorry,' Grace whispered and held Peter tight, hugging him fiercely. 'It's one thing to think like a wolf and quite another to think like a human being.' She stepped around him and looked him in the eyes.

'Those rare moments when I am human, I get thanks to Grizelda. It takes getting used to my body, the feelings, the thoughts. I have to remind myself every day that I am a human trapped inside a wolf's body.'

Peter brushed his fingers over the bare skin of her arm. 'It takes some getting used to, seeing you, the real you again,' he said. 'The last I saw the real you was when you died in my arms. For the third time,' Peter said, his voice barely a whisper.

'Done quarrelling with her, are you?' Grizelda asked from the corner. 'You know, I could rustle up small vials you could carry home,' she offered. 'I've just bought new ones at the market.'

Grace started nodding as Peter still looked puzzled.

'You'll have to make sure nobody else is home, when a giant black wolf comes in and turns into your long-lost wife. Get my drift?'

Grace nodded while Peter still looked skeptical.

'Or do you prefer I leave my humble abode so you can have a bit of a romp now while I'm gone?' Granny winked at the husband and wife who both gaped at her.

When Granny had excused herself just like she had promised, Peter couldn't keep from touching his wife. If he wasn't hugging her, he was holding her hand. Or embracing her shoulders. Or kissing the side of her head.

'I can't believe you're...you,' he said into her neck and inhaled her smell.

'It'll fade soon. I'll be a wolf again.' Grace smiled and ran her fingers through his floppy hair.

'Yes, but you have a chance to be human every once in a while,' he said, pulling her close again.

'For an hour. Until the potion runs out.'

'She'll make more.'

Grace extracted herself, cupped Peter's cheeks and looked deep into his eyes. 'No, Peter. She can't. She didn't make the potion to begin with. And while she's good with herbs, she cannot replicate that cursed potion. We've tried.'

Peter blinked. 'So... You'll be a wolf until the aneurysm bursts again and...?'

'And I am resurrected as me at the Agency and reinserted back here as a wolf. Again.'

'When the potion runs out,' he whispered, eyeing the half-empty purple bulbous bottle in the corner.

'When it runs out.' Grace bit her lip and pressed herself against him. 'That's it.'

'Well, old girl, we don't seem to be able to catch any kind of luck,' Peter mumbled as he gathered her into an embrace.

'Luck.' Grace snorted.

They held each other for a long time.

When he let her go, Grace quickly wiped a tear from the corner of her eye.

'Your eyes...'

'It's okay,' Grace said. 'It'll pass. I'm just sad, that's all.'

'No. Your eyes. They used to be grey. When you were human. If I remember correctly. Your wolf eyes were always green. And they are green now.'

'Are they?' Grace asked, walked over to the corner and yanked off the linen cloth that revealed a bronze gilded mirror. 'Imagine that. They *are* green,' Grace said.

Peter came to stand behind her and put his arms around her. 'I like it. Green or grey. They are yours. I like you, no matter what you look like. I even like you as a wolf.'

Grace turned and found his lips.

When they broke apart to catch their breath, she said, 'I like you, too.'

Peter chuckled. 'Well, judging by the kissing, you more than like me.'

Grace smiled again and felt a twinge in her extremities. 'Peter. I'm about to turn. I can feel it.'

'That's all the time we have?' He let her go.

'Let's just...' Grace said, looking strained.

'Take what we're given,' he finished, seeing her disappear into Granny's bedroom.

18. Embers to Flames

Peter

An hour later, the huntsman was escorted home by the black wolf who occasionally sniffed at the bundle of rabbits hanging over the man's shoulder.

'Can you believe Grizelda, asking if she should leave so we could have a romp,' Peter said to the wolf and patted the vials in his pocket as they walked the path side-by-side. 'It's so strange having this conversation with you, you know. Any conversation.'

'Wait. When. We. Get. There,' the wolf barked.

'It's not like I expect you to leap into my bed the minute you turn human, but I'd like to send Henry to be with Granny overnight. So, we could...talk.'

'Talk.' The wolf barked its throaty laugh.

'Yes, talk. Or do you think I'm so sex starved...'

The wolf shook her head. 'No. Figh-ting.'

The huntsman ran a hand through his hair. 'Sorry, sorry. I'm not picking a fight. That's not what I meant to do at all.'

For a while they both walked in silence. Dusk descended and the woods were settling in for the night. Man and beast fell into step next to each other, the wolf trotting two steps for each step Peter took.

After a while, Peter spoke. 'I've had a lot of time to think, these past two years. When I watched you. The wolf you. I didn't know what to think. I didn't know whether there was any you left in that wolf. I thought you had killed the two sheep straight after you changed, but it turned out it was a young one from the pack that I had to put to death. When I saw you with the pups, I was angry. You seemed so happy, raising someone else's children. Instead of staying with me and Henry. I know you didn't choose to be a wolf, but still. I resented you your freedom, while I was...'

The wolf perked up her ears.

'When I noticed you following Henry around, at first, I thought you might do him harm. You know...not know he was yours. When he told me that you tried to keep him from harm's way, I realized the pups were just substitutes.'

The wolf looked up at him.

'I thought a lot about how you were genuinely surprised when Gabriel came to get you two years ago. You did remember the deal and that you needed to go, but you didn't remember borrowing Morgana's body. I think you must have blocked it out.'

Grace kept listening.

'I remember the first time I found you, lying on our bed, eyes staring at the ceiling with baby Henry crawling all over you, crying. He sensed you were gone. I saw it. Then Henry was alone on the bed. Your body just...disappeared. Then the next minute it was you, looking ten years younger, standing next to me, grabbing for the baby. It was jarring. I felt like I was in a never-ending loop. Except I didn't know when you were going to die next. In the Magic Kingdom, because of how Time moves here, your aneurysm was unstable. Henry was confused and you kept dying. I understand why you agreed to borrow Morgana's body. More durable. But how could you have forgotten about it? That's what I first thought. How could you have fated me to an impossible life - living next to the person I loved and not being able to touch her. Because touching someone else's body would not have been the same. It was never the same.'

The wolf kept listening as Peter's words kept pouring out.

'I hated you a little. After our trysts. You were happy and I felt like I had just cheated on you. I pulled away, busied myself with my newspaper and my articles and my research trips. That's why I was almost never home. For a while, I thought that as it was you who had made the bargain to give Ella her happily ever after in return for a half-life here, with Henry, so it should be you that bears the brunt of that decision. But it was me that was bearing the brunt of it. I was in pain. Part of me still loved you and part of me was cursing you. Until Gabriel took you and made you a wolf forever.'

The wolf's ears twitched and a lone tear trickled into her snout.

'I know it wasn't easy. It was an impossible choice. I agreed that we should make it. I didn't know what was to come. I didn't realize I had started resenting you at some point. I tried so hard not to. But when I saw you turn into a wolf and realized I would never ever get to hold you or smell your hair or hear you laugh or just hold your hand, my heart broke. I felt something snap inside. That night, I held Henry and told him all the good stories about us and you and... I hoped. Against all odds, I hoped and wished out loud that you would come back. That I would give anything if you would only come back. So I could resent you a little less and love you a little bit more and more each day. And now you're here. We are here.'

The huntsman gestured at his house.

'I can't imagine what it must be like, a human mind trapped in a wolf's body for two years. For a while I was afraid that your human mind would eventually dim and your animal instincts would take over. That you would forget me. Forget Henry. Like you forgot about borrowing Morgana's body for three years when yours kept giving out.'

The wolf stood still.

'Should. I. Go?'

'No. Stay,' Peter said. 'I'll send Henry to Granny's.'

The man went inside only to emerge moments later holding a note. 'Henry is helping Greta and they will stay at The Duchess tonight.'

The wolf stayed put.

'Come on in. Turn. Wash. We'll sup. And then you can tell me off about everything I just told you on our walk.' The huntsman smiled mirthlessly.

The wolf slunk inside the house and waited for Peter to open one tiny bulb of purple liquid. After she turned, she briefly appeared, enveloped in a huge towel, squeezed her husband's hand, snatched the satchel with the clothes Grizelda had packed for her and went in search of water to clean up.

Peter busied himself with lighting a fire in the hearth.

'I've had a long time to think about a lot of things as well, darling,' Grace told Peter as soon as she had gotten her bearings. 'How unfair it all must have seemed to you. How patient you were with me. Why you stayed away so much, not wanting to be led into temptation with what you knew to be someone else's body even if I had forgotten this little fact. How amazed I was to realize, in the end that you still...loved me. No matter what. You didn't want to let me go. And I didn't want to go. Deal or no deal.'

The fire crackled and Peter threw a few more logs into its maw.

'Would you like to have dinner?' Peter offered.

'I don't care about dinner. I just want to be with you,' Grace said and enveloped both of them in a blanket as he pulled her onto his lap.

For a long while, nothing was said.

'I understand, the last five years...hell, the last fifteen years have been difficult for you, for both of us,' Grace whispered. 'I know you wanted things to get better here. In a way, they are better, aren't they?' Grace looked up at him.

Peter nodded slowly.

'I know I put you in one impossible situation after another. Trying for a baby for ten years. Dying on you before I had Henry. Relocating not to a different city or country, but a whole new dimension and sticking us all in a fairytale. Switching my body with someone else's, which so ruined the bedroom delights.'

'Oh, those were not ruined. When we managed to...you know.'

'Swine!' She slapped his arm playfully. 'You were cheating on me, may I remind you.' Grace glared at him.

'I was, but who put me in that situation?' He glared right back.

Grace grew serious.

'It was only a few times I touched that body. For me, it was always you. You were always there in your sassy spirit.'

'True, but it was an impossible situation nevertheless,' Grace admitted and put her forehead against his. 'Then to top it all off, I had blocked all memories of the body-switch ever happening and promptly turned into a wolf. Imagine that.'

'Yes, imagine that. Now that *did* put a kibosh on the bedroom delights. For two years, woman,' Peter growled into her neck. 'You've let me go hungry for two years. Well, five, to be honest.' Peter squeezed Grace tight, his hands finding all the soft places.

'Oi, what are you doing?'

'Exploring. I'm allowed. We're married.'

'Married or not, I still expect civilities.' Grace made a pouty face. 'Flowers, dinner, a movie....'

'We went for a nice walk. There were flowers in the woods. I offered dinner. You declined.' Peter raised an eyebrow.

Grace looked mock horrified. 'So walk - check. Flowers - check. Dinner - check. Now sex - check? You're awful.'

'I'm awful and I'm hungry and my body likes you.'

'I think the fifteen years of marriage have atrophied your sweet-talk.' Grace snorted. '"My body likes you?" Seriously?'

Peter wiggled his eyebrows at his wife. 'I could strip. Or you could.'

Grace rolled her eyes. 'It gets better.'

Peter stood up and bowed. 'Care to hum?'

Grace laughed throatily and shook her head. 'You're on your own cowboy.'

'Oh, I hope not.' Peter turned and busied himself with the cords that held the collar of his shirt together. 'Observe.' He yanked the shirt loose and lifted it above his head.

Grace felt her mouth go dry when she saw the taut muscles of his abdomen. Years of living outdoors and her husband was sculpted like a Greek god! The next thing she knew, Peter's shirt flew at her head. She caught it and inhaled his musky scent.

Meanwhile, Peter shimmied his pants loose, holding them up with one hand and trying to rid himself of his boots.

She nearly fell over laughing until his pants dropped and what she saw there was no laughing matter at all. 'My, my, husband dear. I think you're happy to see me.'

'See you, feel you, touch you, give me something!' the man barked and grabbed for her.

She dodged him a couple of times, all the while leading him to the bedroom. When there was nowhere to dodge, Grace produced a tiny bottle from the pocket of her dress, drained it and then took Peter's face into her hands.

She kissed him. Deeply.

He froze for a second. 'I've missed you.'

'Yes,' she breathed, 'Me, too. Now shut up and kiss me. We have an hour.'

'That's a lifetime.'

They never made it to the bedroom. Twenty minutes later they lay exhausted on the living-room rug in front of the fireplace that was spitting embers.

'I thought we…' Peter panted and pointed at each of them in turn, 'were dead.'

'So did I, darling. So did I. Care for another round?'

After another bout of hurried love-making, they lay in front of the hearth and watched the fire die. Grace reached out and threw one more log into the fire pit and fanned the flames. The orange glow licked the wood that lit up, ember by ember and soon roared to life.

'Like us,' Peter said and hugged her.

'Rising from the ashes,' Grace said. 'Embers to flames.'

'Well, if Cinders got her happily ever after, why shouldn't we?' Peter winked at his wife who had crawled away, ready to turn back into a wolf.

19. The Pup

Peter

The next morning, the black wolf emerged from the ferns near the house and darted back only to reappear seconds later.

'Hello, you!' Peter smiled at the beast. 'Up and about so early?'

The wolf charged and pulled him toward the woods by the leg of his trousers.

'You want us to have a nice romp in the woods, darling? How many vials should I bring?'

The wolf snorted and yanked on Peter's trousers, making him sway.

'Lets. Go.'

'Hold on. You're not playing around? Did something happen?' the huntsman asked. Receiving a nod, he hurried inside to get his rifle and headed after the wolf into the forest.

'Where are we going?' Peter asked Grace.

She only growled and coughed, urging him on. The wolf stopped on the edge of a field of wheat. Then she whined.

The huntsman approached. A small fur ball lay at the female wolf's feet, curled up, with one mangled paw in a huge trap. By the markings, Peter recognized it was one of his traps, but he didn't remember setting it here. He also recognized the pup - it was one of the alphas' litter. Peter scanned the forest edge and the fields for any humans.

'Who would take one of my traps and set it near a field?' Peter wondered aloud, kneeling at the pup's lifeless body. 'Did you call for help as soon as he got caught up?'

The wolf shook her head. 'Mis-sing.'

'The pup went missing? So, it wandered off and got trapped and that's how you found him?'

The female wolf howled and the man shushed her. 'Not now. Not safe.'

The huntsman started disentangling the young wolf from the trap, which was crusted over with blood. Then he noticed the angle of the pup's head. There was hardly any blood on his paw. Yet, the trap had crusted blood all over it. Could this be from previous times? Any huntsman knew to clean his traps after removing the prey, but per- haps the villagers were not as knowledgeable?

Had the pup really sprung the trap and before it could bleed to death, had someone broken its neck out of mercy? This could only have happened after the young wolf had struggled himself tired.

There should have been more blood.

The huntsman inspected the pup's head.

Bite marks.

The pup's neck had been broken alright.

By another animal.

Just after the pup had gotten caught in the trap.

Could this have been a mercy kill by his own kind?

But where was the benefactor?

Two things were certain.

The pup had been here a while. And appearances were deceiving.

20. Visitors

Peter

The next day, the wolf stuck her snout through the door minutes after everyone had left the huntsman's abode. For a second, Peter froze and then he reached for one of the vials. He dribbled the concoction over some bread and offered it to Grace.

'Turn. A-way.' The wolf barked before chomping on the bread.

Peter did as he was told. He didn't want to see his wife in pain any more than she wanted to show him.

His eyes downcast, he held up a blanket and felt two human hands seize it.

'Thank you, darling,' Grace said and retreated to the bedroom. 'I'll be a moment.'

Peter started laying out a small luncheon for the two of them. There was a knock on the door, which opened almost immediately.

'Yoo-hoo! Peter! Are you home?'

Peter cursed under his breath and rushed to close the bedroom door.

'I'm here about the wolves.' A man dressed in peasant attire stomped in. 'There are just too darn many of them. First, two sheep were killed a month ago quite like the ones slaughtered a few years back. Now one more has gone missing. What I'm here to tell you is that you have to go hunting.' Only then did the man take in the table set for two and Peter standing with his back to the bedroom.

The man craned his neck. 'Do you have a lady friend there or something?'

When Peter didn't respond, his visitor ploughed on. 'Someone just saw a tawny wolf in the woods that doesn't seem to be afraid of humans. Two sheep are dead and now another sheep is missing.'

'Missing?'

'From an enclosure, no less. One day it was there and the next day it wasn't. We think a wolf carried it off.'

'Was there blood?'

'What?'

'I asked - was there blood in the enclosure? Any sign that the sheep was attacked?' Peter asked.

'No. Why?'

'Wolves don't gently pick up the sheep to carry them off and feast on them later,' the huntsman said.

The villager scratched his stubble.

'Was the enclosure sturdy?' Peter enquired.

'If you mean were there any holes that the critters could have escaped from?' The man patted his neck. 'Naagh, it was sturdy.'

There was coughing from the chamber.

'You do, you do have someone in there. Good lad.' The villager winked. 'And right it is. You've been without a missus for too long.'

The huntsman ignored him and asked, 'Did anyone in the village or neighboring villages happen to have a feast in the last few days, straight after that sheep went missing?'

The villager scratched his jaw. 'Now that you mention it, a neigh- bour a few houses down from where the sheep was taken laid out quite a spread for his only daughter's wedding. They invited half the village for the blessing, although they are not so well off.'

'Any lamb being offered?'

'Why yes, they are a shepherding family, it's proper...'

'Well, there you have it. There was no wolf. Either that neighbor and his wife cooked the sheep or someone else did. Shepherding families are expected to offer lamb. It's more likely that the bride's father did the taking than a wolf carrying the sheep off.'

'So, I suggest you be careful about spreading lies about wolves.' Grace appeared in the doorway of Peter's bedchamber, wearing one of the witch's recognizable colorful skirts.

As the villager gawped, she walked over and pecked Peter on the cheek. 'Darling, I must be going in ten minutes.'

'Wait!' the huntsman and the villager said in unison as Grace went back into the bedroom.

'But I saw a wolf...' the visitor whined.

Peter zeroed in on the man. 'You said someone saw a wolf, now it's you who saw it? Describe it to me.'

The villager glanced at the chamber door that was left ajar. 'Well, it was sort of like a dog, but a big one.'

'Where did you read that? In a children's book?'

'It was reddish. Or it might have been brown.'

Peter frowned. 'Which one was it - reddish or brown? Wolves look as different from each other as people. They, like us, have personalities, they love...'

The villager narrowed his eyes at Peter. 'Are you a huntsman or a wolf-lover?'

A laugh sounded behind the chamber door. 'He isn't, but I am.' The gypsy woman emerged again, looking wilder, her short ink-black hair flying everywhere, her eyes emitting a faint green glow.

'Oh my... You're a...you're a...'

'Witch. You can say it.' Grace smirked. 'Wolves and witches go together, you know. Don't make me call my pet, now.'

The villager retreated toward the door.

'Now... Gr...' Peter started.

'Shhh.' Grace put a finger to Peter's lips and cast him The Look. 'I know perfectly well what my name is. What's yours?' she asked the villager. 'So that I know to tell the wolves whom not to attack for spreading vicious lies about them. But only if you stop doing it.'

'Chuck.' He hiccoughed.

'That's short for Charles, I presume?' Grace asked. 'What a wonderful regal name. Best if you started acting accordingly, don't you think? You've interrupted us long enough, Charles. Peter, I must be on my way.' Grace disappeared into the bedroom.

The huntsman nodded and told Chuck, 'I will check on that rogue in the woods and find out if he has developed a liking for mutton. If it has, I will make sure it's put down. I'll also make sure whoever took the sheep from his neighbor pays for them,' the huntsman promised as he ushered the villager out of his hut.

Chuck stood slack-mouthed for a while until he heard a growl coming from inside the house.

'It's her pet, her pet has come to see her home!' the villager shouted and made a run for it. He didn't even hear the growl turning into a barking laugh.

'I'm. Af-raid. That's. All. We. Have. Time. For. To-day.' The wolf barked.

Peter crouched down beside her. 'Don't go yet.'

'You. Like. To. See. Me. Like. This.' The wolf wagged her tail.

'I wanted to ask you something yesterday. Before you seduced me.' The huntsman winked.

The wolf barked 'Li-ar', earning a raucous laugh and a scratch behind her ear.

'I quite liked our reunion. But I did want to talk to you. Eventually. About the wolves.'

The wolf sat herself down.

'They accept that you go around with Henry. They have accepted you smelling of him. They accepted you, a former human, not an original wolf into their pack. Are the wolves magic? Are they weres?'

The wolf shook her head. 'Trus-ting.'

'Okay. How did you ask them if you could watch over Red? Did you show them? Howl at them? How do you communicate?' Peter asked Grace. 'How do you make yourself understood?'

'Show. Them. Show. Pups. How. To. Hunt. How. To. Track. Why?'

The huntsman looked thoughtful. 'I've seen you do that, leading by example. I've seen the older wolves play and feign defeat to teach young ones what victory feels like. What I have in mind, I cannot show.'

'I-mi-tate.'

'Draw? Will they understand drawing?'

The wolf shrugged.

Peter looked skeptical. 'Why would they listen to me anyway? I doubt I'll be able to get close enough to show I mean no harm before they scatter. I need a plan.' He jumped up and started pacing. 'How could I tell them about what I have in mind...' Peter frowned.

'Tell. Me.'

'I've been taking their dead and passing them off as my kills, as you very well know. They must hate me.' Peter said. 'I'd like to come to some sort of agreement with the pack, that they are okay with me doing this.'

'I. Think. How. To. Ask.' The wolf stood up.

'When will I see you again?'

'To-mor-row. Bring. Hen-ry.'

The wolf wagged her tail, jumped out of the window and disappeared into the forest.

21. The Interrogation

At the palace

The next morning, Prince Nicholas barged into the palace library and closed the double doors behind him. 'Is what mother told Ella true? About our entire bloodline being cursed?'

The man with a full mane of shoulder-length blond hair lifted his head. 'Nicholas. I thought mother already told you about the curse three years ago when you turned eighteen.'

'She told me on the morning of my eighteenth birthday that come midnight, I was going to turn into a hideous beast, but not to fear, she or you would be there to chain me up!' Nick spat as the man cringed. 'Maman said it's *only* from midnight to noon every day until my own son is born and then I could choose not to turn, just like you could after I was born. Mother said that's why she had the masked ball in honor of my eighteenth birthday the night before my actual birthday. But she told me the real reason for having the ball early on the morning of the fête.'

'It was more like lunch, considering the time you woke up,' the king said, finding a speck of non-existent dust on his midnight-blue lapel.

'When mother explained the full extent of my...'

'Our.'

'Our predicament.'

'Be that as it may, now Ella and you have David, you don't have to turn, if you don't want to. As far as I understand, you don't particularly want to?' the king asked.

'Do you?' Nick asked, incredulous.

'I've embraced both my sides, animal and human,' Thomas admitted, inclining his head.

'Embraced?'

'I embraced my beast side fully when I thought I'd lost your mother. Before she became your mother.'

Nick waited for more of an explanation.

The king sighed and put his papers away. 'It's not quite like the fairytale about Beauty and the Beast, which Belle used to read to you at bedtime.'

'There was no enchanting fairy? You were not naughty? There was no curse? No Gustave?'

'Oh, there was a Gustave, alright,' Thomas clenched his jaw. 'And a curse. Cast by an enchantingly decomposing fairy, but what happened wasn't her fault. Not really.'

'I think you'd better tell me the real story, father. Including how the curse mutated when you cast the spell to make you a Beast permanently and why True Love's Kiss didn't work. Or so Ella told me. And why you and mom never had any more kids. I know you wanted to.'

The Beast sighed. 'We can't.'

'You mean you're not able to? Physically?' Nick forced the last word out.

The king shook his head. 'Magically.'

'Meaning?'

'I was cursed already before your mother came into my life. An unfortunate decision to deny a fairy in disguise lodgings for the night. Although I don't blame Caroline. She's not the one who made the curse, she only cast it at someone's request.'

'Caroline? You mean the fabled zombie fairy godmother you kept telling me about was the one who cursed you?' Nicholas asked.

'Cursed me, yes, but she didn't come up with the curse, which is why she also helped me. For that I love and respect her.'

'Although she kept cursing you every night?'

'Well, not quite every night.' The king's eyes sparkled with mischief. 'Let me tell you how I really met your mother. But first, let's go for a walk. We'll change in the woods.' Thomas loosened his cravat.

Nick's face soured.

'Do you want to hear the story or not?' Thomas asked and rose to go. 'There is something I need to check on anyway.'

Nick reluctantly followed. 'Mother told Ella she saw you turn and decided to seek out Morgana to cure you.'

Thomas shook his head. 'I'm sorry, I don't remember much of the time between meeting Belle in the woods and when she came back. When I was Beast full-time.'

Nick looked into his father's eyes, which mirrored his baby-blues, and didn't see even a hint of falsehood. He really didn't remember. 'And you wonder why I don't want to be a Beast. If you forgot everything while you were in animal form, what's to prevent me from forgetting my true essence and tearing someone to shreds? Or killing my own family?' Nick asked.

'That's why you should practice. If you are unsure and alone, you can let Ella or Mother chain you up before you turn. Right now, in the woods, you'll be with me.'

They descended the grand white marbled staircase and headed for the stables. The king's horse was already waiting for him. The stable boy expertly saddled up the prince's favorite steed and they headed for the forest.

As they dismounted near a giant oak, Nick asked, 'Mother mentioned there could have been another solution. Do you remember what it was?'

King Thomas sighed, throwing the reigns over a tree branch. 'That was the last thing I do remember. Because when Belle found out about my beastly side, she left. That broke my heart. I thought I had nothing to lose. So, my godmother and I, we devised a spell to tie my curse to a rose.'

Next, the king stripped to his birthday suit and put his clothes under the oak tree.

Nick saw the king turn into a lion and reluctantly followed suit.

'WHAT HAPPENED? AND why are we going this convoluted way?' Nick enquired when they had zig-zagged in the underbrush for a while, the straight and narrow forest path long forgotten.

'We need to stay downwind. Or they will smell us.'

'They?'

'The wolves.'

'Oh, we're playing the hunting game. Got it!' The younger lion hunched down and tried to tread lightly. After five minutes he gave up and rose to his usual level. 'Did you...'

'Shush!'

Nick resorted to whispering, 'Did you manage to woo Mother in your Beast form, just like the story-book says?'

The older lion tossed his mane. 'No. I wooed Belle in my human form. Because I turned human at midday on the day following her arrival. And then again into a Beast at midnight. Morgana's counter-curse had started working and it undid Caroline's permanent spell. But your mother still insisted that because of my delicate sensibilities where romance is concerned, I woo her before we marry.'

'Considering I'm twenty, almost twenty-one now and you are thirty-nine, it took you...six months to woo Maman?' The prince looked into the crisscross irises of his father. 'But I thought your kiss was a True Love's Kiss? You became human the next day.'

'Yes, but even if the curse knew that deep down your mother and I loved each other, we wanted to know and feel it and remember it, too. You have to admit, it would be awkward to go from meet to marry in a day.'

'So, you wooed her.'

'So, I wooed her. Now, shush.'

The two beasts crept closer to the caves the wolves had chosen for their lair. 'Observe,' Thomas told Nick.

The younger lion scanned the scene. Pups were playing with the older wolves. Crows hopped about. A young wolf pair was sniffing each other in the ferns, away from the prying eyes of the pack.

'What are we looking at? Why did we come here?' Nick whispered.

'We are not the only ones observing the pack.' The older lion motioned with his head.

'Do you mean that black wolf who is playing with the pups?' Nick asked. 'She stands out.'

'No. She just looks different, but they have long since accepted her. I meant that tawny one in the ferns,' the king said.

'The one sweet-talking the young female? That's just young love.' Nick tried to smile and found it was awkward in lion form.

The older lion shook his head. 'In a wolf pack, young love is always a rather open affair. These two are hiding.'

'Maybe he's just the omega?' Nick offered.

'That's just a rubbish human concept of a lowly underling everyone uses for a punching bag. Wolves are very fair creatures. No. That reddish one is not part of that pack.'

'How do you know?'

'While he's necking with the female, he's doing exactly what we are doing. He's observing.'

Nick took a long hard look and saw what his father had noticed. The russet wolf had chosen a spot where he could see the whole pack. Despite the affectionate nudges he was giving the female, his snout remained trained toward the wolves as if pulled by a magnet. He was looking in one direction and one direction only.

'Do you think he's up to something?'

AFTER THEIR SCOUTING trip, Nick and Tom headed back to where they had left their clothes. 'Obviously, Mother came back or else I wouldn't be here,' Nick said, donning his shirt. 'And given that I can shift, I'm definitely not adopted.'

'You nearly weren't born. When I saw Belle after being a beast for two years, I almost ate her. We had such a row!' Thomas said.

'Ate her?!? What do you mean you almost ate her?' Nick's eyes goggled.

'Well, her charming directness and insistence on taking things into her own hands had taken itself to a whole new level when in the employ of Morgana, the Fairy Queen.'

'Oh, do tell,' Nick asked, so Thomas did.

22. The Rogue

Peter

The huntsman followed the trail. Large paw marks. Two sets. Large cats.

'You can come out now, Your Majesty,' Peter said.

Two lions emerged from the shadows.

'Hello, Peter.'

'Hello, Tom. Hello, Nicholas. Hunting?'

'Walking. Teaching Junior here the wild ways.'

The smaller lion nudged his father's shoulder.

'Tell me, have you noticed anything strange in the forest as of late?' the king asked Peter.

'Anything strange?' Peter echoed.

'I've seen wolves do strange things. One lone wolf in particular. And it's not the black female. There is a new tawny one about.'

Peter cocked his head. 'What did you see?'

'He's spying on the wolf pack. Avoiding the traps you have set as if he knows where they all are. Seducing a young female on the sly,' Thomas listed off.

Peter chewed it over. 'Wolves only spy on rival packs and humans. As for avoiding my traps - the only way someone would know about them is if they had seen me set them. I'm not liking the sound of a rogue wolf spying on me.'

'That is irregular, right?' The younger lion asked and saw his elders nod.

'What are you going to do about it?' Thomas asked.

'I'll find a way to let the pack know,' the huntsman assured him.

The lion made a suggestion, 'I'd change up your routine, if I were you.'

The huntsman nodded. 'The rogue might know who my nearest and dearest are if he has been following me around.'

'Expect trouble,' the king said. 'How can you warn the pack? I've been happy to keep myself to surveying, but I could interfere, if you want.'

'The black female,' Peter said. 'I'll...talk to her. Although she is an outsider, the pack will listen to her.'

'Not if she doesn't have actual proof. And she doesn't.'

'The actual proof might already be there. We're just being slow connecting the dots,' Peter's face darkened as he remembered the dead wolf pup.

'Meaning?' Nicholas chimed in.

'Are you aware that a few sheep have gone missing in the village? Two years ago, and again just recently. A few days ago, Gr...I found a dead pup in one of my traps where I hadn't set it. The pup's neck had been snapped. By an animal,' Peter reported. 'It was the son of the alphas.'

'The alphas?' The lion looked as if he was deep in thought. 'Tell me, this spring, how many pups have the alphas managed to raise?'

'None. Only two were born and both are dead, one of them under rather suspicious circumstances. Why?' Peter asked.

'I'd say someone doesn't want the ruling pair procreating.' Nicholas glanced at his father for confirmation.

'Even if both pups did not meet their ends by accident, what's the point of killing the sheep?' Peter asked.

'Practice runs for killing larger prey perhaps. Or inciting the humans against the pack to stir trouble,' King Thomas offered.

Peter looked deep in thought. 'You think the rogue wolf is planning a coup?'

The lion nodded. 'I think the alpha male is going to find himself challenged.'

'If there is a challenge and if the alpha male is seriously injured, the alpha female would probably pick a strong new pair to lead the pack. She would not accept the outsider who stirred up trouble,' Peter argued.

'Yes, but what if the outsider who has challenged and defeated the alpha pairs up with one of the young females in the pack? If you add up the pups and the sheep...when the pack is in havoc, the wise and humble newcomer who has been insinuating himself into the trust of some of the young ones will step up. That's how I would do it,' the king mused.

'Are you absolutely sure?' Peter asked.

The lion nodded.

'Thank you, Your Majesty. You've given me food for thought. And a task to check out the newcomer. Much appreciated. Happy walking to you both.'

Nick

'WHY DID YOU LET ELLA'S father in on the secret?' Nick asked as they emerged from the forest on horseback. 'Only mother and Ella know.'

'Them and half the castle. The villagers still call me Beast. They would be surprised if they didn't see me turn.' The king chuckled.

'Yes, but why Peter? I'm sure Ella would never tell. Did you think he'd kill us, if he didn't know it was us?'

'It's his forest,' Thomas said. 'Peter has long since known the lions are royals in disguise. He can track us by our prints. As for danger, he would never kill a creature unless it was for food,' the king said. 'This huntsman, unlike the previous one, is an ally who can keep a secret. You would do well to remember this, Nicholas. For future purposes.'

The prince nodded and mumbled, 'I thought this was our forest.'

When they reached the stables, the king dismounted, dropped the reigns to a stable boy and fixed his amber eyes on his son. 'Nick, you would also do well to remember that ownership has more to do with responsibility than power. Ownership papers would mean nothing, if you were caught in a trap in the forest. In the wilderness, the power lies with its inhabitants and the person who knows the lay of the land like the back of his hand.'

King Thomas let his words sink in. 'Knowledge is power.'

Peter

A FEW HOURS LATER, the huntsman was clinging to a branch of his favorite lookout tree, keeping very still. He had never seen one wolf spy on another before. Two years ago, the black female had been hesitant, but open about approaching the pack. Not this brownish rogue, though. He was following the leader of the pack upwind, cowering in the ferns.

Peter had never seen this russet male before. This must be the wolf Tom had mentioned.

A stray?

Wolves were very territorial. Strays were usually not tolerated. Either the pack chased them away or killed them on sight, especially when they were males.

The pack had accepted Grace, although she didn't have a cub. A wolf cub, anyway. Had it been the welcome the pups had given Grace that had made the pack accept her?

The tawny rogue wolf crawled on his belly to the next cops of ferns.

Was he practicing how to show humility before he revealed himself to the alpha male?

The huntsman doubted it.

Two years ago, Grace had done it in a different manner. She had come out into the open on a vast meadow at the edge of the forest, the wolves' hunting ground, waited for the sentinel to alert the entire pack and stayed in the meadow to show that she was alone. She had just stood there for half a day until the pack had gathered and watched her and had sent an emissary to chase her off. A few days later she had returned with a cub. Not her own. The pack's. He figured the pup had strayed into the forest, Grace had found it and had come to return it. The cub had bounded up to his parents and back to Grace. When the pup's mother had sniffed the black wolf over and hadn't bared its teeth at her, Peter had guessed the vetting process was completed. Without many introductions, the pack had turned their backs and Grace had followed them, unimpeded, the saved cub and its siblings prancing around her.

It was rare for the pack to accept strangers.

Peter was sure the pack would never accept this solitary male. He would have to contend for leadership to stay. If the rogue killed the alpha male of the pack, he would still have the alpha female to worry about.

People always thought leadership with wolves was up to one wolf. Mistakenly and due to the patriarchal preference in human society, the grey male would have been suspected of being the leader.

With wolves, it was always a pair that led the pack – an alpha male and an alpha female – who took decisions together. When in doubt, the huntsman had seen the male defer to the female. The alphas took charge when danger hit. Only then would they turn up at the front, leading. Like the time he had seen the pack hunting and they had hit an unfamiliar scent. The alphas had taken the lead and explored until they had found the bear tearing up a deer carcass. They had led the pack away from trouble. Any other time, they were comfortable to share leadership, allowing any wolf from the pack to assume responsibility for a while.

In any case, he might have a dead wolf on his hands very soon. He would put the cadaver to good use, as always, to appease the villagers. He just hoped it wasn't a wolf he cared about.

If the rogue wanted to challenge the leading pair, Peter was sure that should the alpha male die, the female alpha would carry on leading the pack. Until either a new male whom she could accept appeared or until the leadership was passed on, not necessarily by bloodline, to another strong pair who was capable of looking after the welfare of them all. The alpha female would never accept the rogue just because he dared challenge the leader.

The tawny wolf crept closer to the resting silver alpha male and bared his teeth, making no sound.

Peter threw a pine cone, making the rogue scurry off.

For now.

By the looks of it, the pack was about to be subjected to a hostile takeover.

23. The Threat

Henry

Henry grabbed the picnic basket Greta had prepared for Granny and almost ran down the path. After the rain, the forest was always so lush and inviting. And he hadn't seen Wolfie in days! Papa's words from last night still rang in Henry's ears. 'From now on, you don't go into the woods alone, Henry. Only with me or with Granny or with Hans.'

When he had asked what about his black wolf, Papa had relented and said he could go with her as well.

The boy kept glancing left and right to see if his wolf was there. He hadn't seen her or Granny in a while and he couldn't sit and wait for Papa to come home.

Surely there was no danger in the forest during daytime?

When he was half-way to Granny's house, Henry noticed that he hadn't seen a single deer or rabbit dart by.

Henry pulled on the sleeves of his red hoodie and perked up his ears.

The woods were silent. The birds were not chirping. There wasn't a squirrel in sight.

The boy picked up his pace.

Feeling someone watching him, Red turned around, hoping to see his guardian.

'Wolfie?'

Two glowing eyes peered at him from the underbrush. They were a few inches lower than where the black wolf's head usually appeared. And the eyes were entirely the wrong color. They were yellow.

'My what big eyes you have,' Red whispered, scanning the path for stones. There were none.

The eyes blinked and appeared to sink even lower.

'My, what big ears you have,' Red said, louder this time, groping for the loaf of bread in his basket.

Seeing the eyes sink lower still and fidget from side to side, Red threw the loaf at the ferns with all the force he could muster.

Granny had said that throwing doesn't happen in nature and it surprises the animals.

He saw a brownish tail and hind legs dart back into the woods.

The boy took a few tentative steps, picked up his basket and quick marched to Granny's.

When Henry arrived at the hut he was out of breath. He put the basket down on the steps and doubled over. 'Sorry-about-the-bread,' he exhaled.

'What bread?' Granny asked. 'Why have you been running, Red?'

Henry took a few long breaths and finally managed, 'There was a wolf. In the woods. It stared at me like it was about to jump at me, but I threw the loaf of bread at it and scared it away. Then I made lots of noise, sang and beat trees with a stick and ran the last few hundred yards here. Just like you taught me.'

Granny cursed under her breath and her eyes darted to the forest. 'Come in, come in. We'll have to tell your m...your wolf. We will have to tell your wolf.'

'Do you think my wolf is okay, Granny?' Red asked.

'Bless, you almost got jumped and you're worried about your wolf?' Granny hugged Henry close. 'I'm sure she'll come to protect you when you have to go back home, don't fret. From now on, no meandering alone. Either you wait for your wolf to guard you home or ask your father or Hans or me, got it?'

The boy nodded. 'I'm sorry about the bread, though.'

'Forget about the bread,' Grizelda tousled his hair. 'I'll ask the table cloth for new bread. I'm so glad you are alright.'

The old woman hugged him again.

'I can't ask the table cloth for a new Henry, you know,' she said, making him smile

Peter

'GRAN-NY. SAID. NEW. Wolf. Threa-te-ned. Hen-ry. Guard. Him.' Grace barked at Peter in her wolf form before she ran back into the forest.

Peter went inside to get his rifle. It was as he had feared. The rogue knew Henry was his son.

The newcomer was getting troublesome.

Peter didn't believe for a minute that the tawny wolf had been following Henry out of curiosity.

Wolves were curious, yes. But they were always cautious. They never came close to a human, if they could help it. Stayed downwind. Hid in the underbrush. Avoided humans who could harm them.

If a wolf other than Grace was following a human child, he was up to no good.

Grace had told him to guard Henry. That meant she was going to investigate. Peter checked his rifle and put a pack of bullets into his satchel. While Henry was at Granny's, he was safe. And while he was safe, Peter would do well to do some investigating of his own.

24. A Little Payback

Grace

The black wolf growled when she entered the witch's hut and didn't see Henry.

'Where. Is. He.'

'Oh, relax. Hans is taking Henry to Greta,' Grizelda said. 'I doubt the wolf who tried to attack Henry would dare try it with Hans around or go to the restaurant in the village.'

The wolf slunk into the bedroom.

When Grace emerged, wearing a man's shirt and pants, she asked Grizelda, 'No skirts?'

'All in the wash,' the witch said. 'Peter took my other gypsy skirt so you'd have something to wear at his place. Not that you'd need clothes there.' Grizelda winked.

'Come with me to the woods,' Grace begged the old woman.

'Why did you waste the potion if all you wanted to do was go back to the underbrush?' The witch *huffed*.

Grace cocked her head. 'The rogue wolf who has been following Henry - somehow, he has managed to avoid me in my wolf form. I want us to go look for him. As humans. Maybe if he's not afraid of people, he'll do something stupid.'

'Something stupid like gobble one of us up?' Grizelda narrowed her eyes at Grace.

'The potion is likely to wear off by the time we reach the caves. When I'm a wolf again, I can take him, don't worry.'

'It's the one hour you're in your human form that I'm worried about,' the witch countered.

'Well, if you have a better plan, I'm listening,' Grace said.

'Actually, I do,' the witch said and unsheathed her antique mirror.

'Mirror, mirror on the wall, show me Henry, rogue and all.'

The surface of the mirror showed static and then Henry appeared, tugging at Greta's apron strings, begging her for something.

'He has reached The Duchess,' Grace commented. 'Thank you.'

The mirror fogged over and then showed them a sleeping brown wolf at the edge of a cave.

'He's picked out a cave. He's planning a family!' Grace exclaimed. 'And by the looks of it, I know where that cave is!' She started tugging on the older woman's skirt. 'Let's go. Catch him and...'

'And what? Give him a whoopin'?' Grizelda smirked. 'Yeah, I can see it, two women beating up a wolf in the middle of the forest. Nu-uh.'

'If we go there, if humans go there, the cave will no longer be safe and he can't live there and he would have to find a new place and post- pone his procreating plans. He can't have one of our young females! I won't let him!'

'My-my, you're quite the possessive sister to those pups, aren't you,' Grizelda *tsk-tsk*-ed, but started gathering up her satchel nevertheless. 'I've been meaning to pick some wild lavender anyway,' she mumbled.

When they passed the huge pine at the edge of the forest, Grizelda sighed.

'You don't have to come, if you don't want to,' Grace said.

'It's not that,' the witch replied and patted the trunk of the pine. 'Have I ever told you what happened to the "kind" stranger who could be my Mellie's baby-daddy?' Grizelda asked.

Grace shook her head.

The witch nodded with a satisfied look about her. 'That slimy cad got his comeuppance right under this pine tree.'

'What did you do? Turn him into a frog?' Grace asked and Grizelda smirked.

'You did? You turned him into a FROG?!?' Grace looked aghast.

Grizelda tilted her head. 'Let me see... A handsome stranger happened by my hut. He had food, I had booze, we had a jolly good time. The morning after, he was gone, without even a note. When one month later I was puking my guts out, I realized it wasn't the forest mushrooms, and was probably because of that jolly good time we had. That, or it was Oleg's to begin with and I was knocked up already when I arrived here. When I was sure I was pregnant, I made a wish.' Grizelda looked wistfully toward the forest. 'I think it went something like this... If this random dude *is* the father of my child and he is out there somewhere and if he is feeling even a smidgen guilty or slimy about that night and taking advantage of me and skipping out on me the next morning, then may that ounce of ick in his soul multiply so much so that it turns his slimy ass into a frog. Yes, I believe that was it.' The old woman looked like a cat that had got the cream.

'You cursed him?'

'No, I made a wish. There is a difference. Although, not much. With wishes - if you tap into the right thing inside a person or being, and...I guess...activate it...or something... Then your wish comes true,' Grizelda said. 'That's how I've figured anyway. That's how it used to work on Earth. Now enough chit-chat, what were you going to do once you reach the caves?'

'I hope the rogue is still there and I can get close enough,' Grace said.

'And then what? You haven't quite thought it through, have you?' Grizelda asked. 'If you go to the caves in your human form and evict all the wolves, where will they live? And even if you turn into a wolf by the time we reach there, what are you going to do to him when you have that meddler where you want him?'

Grace *hunhed* and for a while they walked the path in silence.

Suddenly, the older woman stopped, counted a few steps out loud and turned left at a cop of ferns. 'Follow me.'

'But that's not in the direction of the caves, Grizelda,' Grace pointed out.

'Not when you're human, it isn't. Have you thought about why the villagers have trouble locating the wolves and killing the whole pack? Why they enlisted Peter to be the huntsman? As humans, they can't find their way in the woods.'

'Are you saying the woods are enchanted? But I can always find my way in the woods,' Grace argued.

'In your wolf form, yes. I guess the enchantment only applies to humans, then,' the older woman speculated.

'How come you can find your way?'

Grizelda winked. 'Goddess, remember? Not entirely human.'

Grace nodded, making her way through the ferns and brambles. Her sense of logic kept screaming that they were going back toward the village, but she told logic to zip it and followed her friend.

For a while, they waded through the underbrush in silence.

'How do you know he turned into a frog?' Grace asked.

'Mellie's baby-daddy?' the older woman asked. 'I heard a croak in the woods after I made the wish, went to look and found his discarded clothes and satchel and a frog sitting amidst it all looking almost as guilty as it looked reproachful.' Grizelda veered off in a zig-zag motion that made Grace smile until she noticed the old woman's eyes were closed.

'You're traipsing blind here?' Grace had to ask.

'Shh, you'll spook my intuition. I always find my way by listening to my intuition. It helps not to see where I'm going.'

Grace tried to do the same for a few minutes, but gave up for fear of losing sight of Grizelda who kept wading and ducking under fallen branches and caressing trees. From the back, it almost seemed like the witch was carrying out some sort of a pagan dance ritual.

When the silence between them got too peaceful, Grace asked, 'Are you sure the frog didn't just happen on the site while the man turned into...something...someone else?'

'The clothes were intact and he was sitting right in the middle of them, almost under them. Werewolves turn by ripping their clothes to shreds. That frog had been a man. Judging by the clothes, the very same man who I had partied with. I guess he was coming back to the hut for some more vodka and fun and I caught his guilty thoughts by the tail and voilà!'

'That's some powerful voilà,' Grace mused to Grizelda's back. 'So, Mellie, Ella, Hans and Greta, they all get their powers from you?'

'Well, that cad could have something to do with it. He's the only unknown variable.' Grizelda twirled around a birch tree. 'This way!' She pointed and they continued their trek.

Grace nodded to herself. 'You know, because of Ella's telepathic powers, for a second there I thought she was the daughter of a guardian angel. Are you sure Ella doesn't get her abilities from her father?' Grace asked.

Grizelda shook her head, sending her hair flying. 'I've met Ozzy, Mellie's good for nothing "Wizard" as he likes to call himself. There isn't an ounce of magic in him, just technical contraptions, so besides the ability to take Mellie places by using portals, I didn't see the allure when she brought him home to meet me. Once. Not that he knew that he was meeting the parents. It was nice that she did, though.'

'So, all we know is that Ella's granddad was someone who *might* have had certain powers?'

Grizelda hugged another tree and whispered something to it. 'I don't have telepathy, so it could be inherited from that...that frog. I did wonder, how he was able to make me...happy... so many times. He might have read my mind and known exactly what to do and what not to do. The arrogant bastard.'

'I thought you didn't remember anything?' Grace asked and Grizelda *hunhed*.

'That I remember.' Suddenly, the older woman stopped and winced.

'What happened? Did you hurt yourself? Are we walking too quickly?' Grace asked.

'No. I just realized... I mean, I hoped that all their powers are manifestations of Luck, but they can't be, can they? Mellie's glamouring, Ella's telepathy... If the cad is Mellie's dad, then she's the living proof I cheated.'

'On your married lover,' Grace said. 'Who might never find out about it. Or are you planning to take Mellie and the rest of them with you when you go back?'

Grizelda shook her head.

A few more trees later, the witch broke the silence. 'Angels have telepathy, huh? I wouldn't know. I've never met one,' Grizelda said.

'Well, I have,' Grace said. 'And they can read minds. It's downright creepy.'

Could Mellie really be the daughter of a guardian angel? It would be ironic, if she had to stepmother the descendants of the person who cursed her to be a wolf.

Grace narrowed her eyes at Grizelda. 'Describe him to me,' she said.

'He was dignified, regal-looking even, very good reflexes,' Grizelda said, remembering the toppled goblet the stranger had caught with ease. 'Also, I think he had Indian blood in him, Asian Indian, not Native American, he had dark brown eyes like liquid toffee, pearly teeth, salt and pepper hair and his hands... They were smooth like velvet.' Grizelda glided to and fro, lost in her memories.

Grace said, 'If you tell me he had questionable ethics...'

Grizelda whipped round. 'Meaning? Dirty jokes or something?'

'No, the angel I'm thinking of could defend even atrocious deeds,' Grace said, remembering the man who could be kind to her when he wanted to and devoid of empathy when he chose.

Grizelda furrowed her eyebrow. 'Now that you mention it. We did discuss my exile. After we had a few, I started ranting about the injustice of it all and that's where we almost fell out, truth be told. He tried to tell me that what Fate did by putting me in this place without a chance of escape for forty years was proportionate to the magnitude of my wish and not evil at all. That was his response after I told him I wanted to strangle Fate for what she had done.'

'Sounds like someone I used to know.'

'Really?'

Grace nodded. 'I don't know his name. I always knew him as the Boss. He used to run the Agency of Guardian Angels before Gabriel took over. Before he *made* Gabriel take over. He was the chiefest angel of them all. Right after, he went to tour the dimensions and has...not been seen since.' Grace fell quiet.

Grizelda started laughing manically and then hiccoughing. In between the clucks, she issued, 'I,' cluck, 'turned,' cluck, 'a deity,' cluck, 'into' cluck, 'a frog!'

'Why deity? I don't think Gabriel's Boss is a deity. Why do you?'

Grizelda inclined her head. 'Boss of all the Guardian Angels, hello?'

Grace exhaled a long sigh. 'Ah. Do you think he's still a frog? How long do frogs live anyway?'

'In Magic Kingdom, things can live for eons,' Grizelda said, motioning for them to continue.

'Or die three days in a row,' Grace mumbled. 'Assuming he's still alive. And you've been here thirty-six years?'

Grizelda nodded.

'That is pretty mean payback.' Grace smiled.

Grizelda turned and returned her smile. Then she noticed a scrap of white linen hanging on a low branch. 'Not another one. Keep a lookout for a girl lost in the woods, will you, Grace?'

'You think someone's lost in the woods?' Grace asked.

Grizelda nodded, holding up the linen scrap. 'You know, over the years I've had to rescue quite a few maidens wandering in these tricky woods, quite a few of them returning from the marshes. They were in right states, too. I didn't press them about what possessed them to go to the marshes alone. They could have been cranberry or cloudberry picking, for all I know.' The witch frowned. 'But if I seem to remember correctly, I think one of those lost girls let it slip that she should never have believed the stupid stories about enchanted princes.'

Grace brightened. 'An enchanted prince? In the marshes? Do you think that girl meant the story of the Frog Prince?'

The witch looked surprised. 'Do you think that's him? Mellie's baby-daddy? Trying to get out of his predicament?'

'How?'

Grizelda rolled her eyes. 'By trying to get the maidens to kiss him, of course!' She said as Grace felt her transformation start.

Half an hour later, they reached their destination. Grizelda had no trouble urging Grace to lie down on her stomach in the underbrush a good hundred paces from the caves.

'Is that the brownish fiend over there?' Grizelda whispered. 'I'm sorry it took us so long to find our way.' The older woman patted Grace on her head. 'The brownish wolf seems to be sticking like glue to his new lady-love. He's courting. Maybe he intends to join the pack?'

Grace emitted a low growl.

'Oh, I know you don't like it, but other people's or wolves' personal life is not strictly your business.'

'It. Is. If. He. Is. Af-ter. Hen-ry.'

'You do have a point. I think this one has *amore* on his brain, not hunting human children. If you want to spy on him some more, go ahead. I'm heading back, if it's all the same to you. Pop by when you're done. Keep me company,' Grizelda said and crawled behind a tree, sitting up to tie her long grey hair into a bun. 'I'm downwind, don't worry, they won't sense me.' Grizelda sneaked off, blending into the forest tapestry with her green peasant dress.

If the wolves noticed a human woman retreating from their grounds, they didn't show it.

25. Three Rocking Pigs

At the hut

After Grace had made sure courtship was the only thing on the rogue's mind, she returned to Grizelda's hut.

When Grace emerged from Grizelda's bedroom, she was met with 'You're alive?'

Grace cringed, looking at the newcomer emanating a familiar sickly-sweet perfume. 'Mellie!' Grace felt her resentment resurfacing as she saw her old nemesis advancing.

Mellie's sour looks matched Grace's feelings.

Grizelda started pouring tea onto her linen table cloth. As per usual, a cup materialized out of thin air and absorbed the libation.

The divine apparition in all things purple turned to Grizelda and pointed a finger at Grace. 'Why is she alive? She can't be alive! She was branded the evil stepmother and evicted from the kingdom. Have you been harboring fugitives, mother?' Mellie made a *faux* gasping noise, bringing her hand to her mouth.

'Oh, stop with the theatrics, Mellie. Remember, we know you well.' The witch intoned.

'Nobody is harboring me.' Grace interjected.

Mellie put up her palm. 'I'm not talking to you. You're the evil stepmother who almost cost Ella her happily ever after.'

Grace rolled her eyes. 'You should know better than to believe the stories you spread, Mellie.'

The woman *huffed*. 'Don't call me that! It's Melisandra, thank you very much! And I'm not spreading anything except happiness and hope.'

'Yes, you are and you know it. Tea?' Grizelda offered a cup to her daughter who took it and stretched out her pinky.

The old woman snorted.

'Well, since you have company for the night, I'll be going,' Grace said, motioning toward the forest.

'Yes, you crawl back under whatever rock you came from and don't come back!' Mellie spat and mumbled, 'Knowing you're alive is bad enough...'

'Manners!' Grizelda admonished.

After Grace had exited through the back door, Grizelda turned to Mellie. 'Now was that necessary? What do you have against Grace? She helped your daughter marry a prince at a considerable expense to her own reputation, while you were not exactly helping. Why are you mad at her for doing right by your child?'

Before Mellie could answer, a will-o'-the-wisp thin girl with auburn hair burst into the hut saying 'Granny! I was able to land the Three Rocking Pigs!' The young girl squealed and pulled Granny into a hug.

'Is that a band?' Granny asked.

'A band? I guess you can call an assembly of three musically-gifted persons a band,' Greta mused, still clinging to her Granny. 'They played at Ella's wedding, remember?'

'I was never invited,' Grizelda reminded her as Greta let go. 'My reputation was cleared and relations with you kids restored publicly *after* Ella was married.'

'Oh, yes, I forgot.' Greta bit her lip. 'In any case, they're coming to play at The Duchess this Friday night. Isn't that amazing!' Greta took Granny's hands and tried to twirl her. Only then did she notice someone else seated at the long table.

'Oh, hello. I didn't know you had company, Granny.' Greta joy deflated. 'Hello, Aunt Mellie.'

'I...I have to be going now. It was nice to see you, sweetie,' Mellie purred at Greta and gone she was.

'Well, that was rude!' Granny frowned.

'I don't mind,' Greta said. 'She doesn't want me sensing her.'

'What do you mean?'

Greta shrugged and put her basket of goodies on the table. 'For you. Leftovers from The Duchess. I wasn't going to...' she lifted a finger to her temple, 'tap into her, you know.'

When Granny raised an eyebrow, Greta explained, 'I don't like feeling that regret and anxious combo Mellie has about her whenever she sees me or Hans. She's calmer around Ella, not so much around me.'

'You're clairsentient.' Granny told the girl.

'What's that?' Greta's eyes lit up.

'You can sense what someone is feeling. Maybe even sense other things, too.'

The witch eyed the girl for a long time. Finally, she asked, 'You know, don't you?'

Greta shrugged. 'You mean that she's my mother? Sure. Her glamours have never worked on me.'

'Never?' Granny looked surprised.

'Never.' Greta took an apple from the basket, looking for Granny's approval beforehand. 'I must admit, I was rather surprised when Mother came back after being absent for four months and said she was our Aunt Mellie. At first, I thought it was a game. But when Hans and Ella started calling her Auntie in earnest and it became clear that they saw her differently to how I did, I realized she was glamouring us on purpose.'

Granny pulled Greta into a close hug. 'And still, you love her. Despite everything. Despite her leaving you and Hans in the woods when you were five, abandoning you when you were ten, pretending that she wasn't your mother...'

Greta shrugged. 'How do you know I still love her, no matter what she's done?'

The witch stroked her hair. 'When you love Mellie, you see through her glamour, that's why you see her for who she really is. When you don't love her, you don't see the real her and she appears a stranger. Any stranger she thinks you'll like. She was gone for a long time. And you and Hans were only ten. Maybe Ella and Hans forgot her and that's why they saw her as "Aunt Mellie" when she returned?'

'Mellie must have her reasons for going away and for keeping away from us. Everybody has reasons. Usually good ones,' Greta said. 'Even if I don't know what my reason for loving her is. Even if I don't know why she doesn't love me.'

'How old are you again? A hundred?' Granny asked and took the girl's hand. 'You're kind and empathic and practically running The Duchess by yourself at age fifteen. You don't need validation from Mellie. Never did.'

'Oh, stop, you're making me cry,' Greta said and blushed.

'You know, it was a clever idea to rename the restaurant after Grace...disappeared.' Granny said.

'Hans tinkered with the sign and amended "Grace's" to "The Graceful Duchess". But everyone shortened it to "The Duchess",' Greta said. 'About that, Hans is helping me tonight, but we have a large crowd...'

'With a band, there's bound to be a crowd.' Grizelda nodded. 'Do you need extra hands to help you serve?'

'Yes, please,' Greta said. 'I'll be doing the serving. Hans can keep the crowds at bay and if you could mix and pour the drinks, maybe that won't be too taxing?'

'I can also help with the seating. Ever since Ella left, I think you're missing a maître d´, aren't you?' Granny asked.

Greta blushed. 'I... The Blue Fairy taught me a spell that directs newcomers to their designated table. Menus are already laid out, so I don't need anyone fronting the restaurant.'

'Spells, huh?' Was all the witch said. 'Apprenticing, are you? You know, it's another curious coincidence that a powerful new fairy appeared in our Kingdom, straight after Grace turned...was turned away from her home. And just like that, the Blue Fairy appears and becomes the local potions master. And you tell me she knows proper magic and is willing to teach it to you?' Granny asked.

Greta smiled and nodded, her head bobbing up and down quickly and eagerly. 'She does! And she is kind and lovely and....'

'Greta, you think everyone is kind and lovely.' The old woman smiled. 'I have a feeling they'll be coming in droves to The Duchess once you master magic to enhance your culinary delights.'

'Until I do, I need other kinds of entertainment. Hence, the pigs.'

'Three little pigs...' the older woman mused, tapping her nose.

'Three Rocking Pigs,' Greta corrected her.

'Yes, yes, that may very well be what they call themselves now, but I'm pretty sure they started from much humbler beginnings,' the witch said. 'Hang on.' Granny went in search of something. She returned with a leathery volume that she laid on the table and turned around for Greta to see.

'Grace's fairytale book!' Greta looked delighted.

'Yes, and whatever she wrote in there seems to be coming true,' Granny said and pointed at a page. 'Read the story.'

Greta did.

When she had finished reading, Greta looked amused. 'So that's their backstory. I always wondered.'

'What did you always wonder, honey?'

'Why Naf-Naf, Nif-Nif and Nuf-Nuf always travel with a wolf as their bodyguard. I guess playing at taverns takes care of feeding them and their wolf, so they can live a life of leisure. Clever little pigs,' Greta said. 'If those are the same pigs, I mean.'

'Do you know any other pigs that are chummy with wolves?' Granny smirked. 'They're the same pigs. I also know a wolf who would sell her soul for pancakes, just like a wolf from another story in this book.' Granny looked deep in thought.

'But how?' Greta asked. 'Did Grace hear these stories and just write them down?'

'No. Grace wrote those stories four years ago. Maybe five. When did the pigs start touring with their band?'

'About three years ago?' Greta looked hesitant. 'Still, how?'

'What you're really asking is why are these stories coming to life,' Granny said. 'The answer is because Grace wrote them down and now I am reading these stories to Henry over and over and over again. The pigs and the wolf story - these are his favorites. That and the dragon stories,' Granny said.

Greta and Granny stared at each other.

'Henry makes things come to life,' Granny said. 'It's the only logical explanation.'

'It could just be a coincidence,' Greta offered.

'Uh-uh. Coincidence my elbow. Just like it's a coincidence that Gr...someone else can successfully use a potion intended only for me,' Granny muttered, nodding at the half-empty purple bottle in an alcove. 'Too bad it'll be running out soon...'

'Potion? What potion? You're running out? Do you need more? Maybe I can help? Greta brightened. 'Well, I can ask the Blue Fairy if she can help.'

Granny eyed her grandchild and nodded very slowly. 'And just like that I stumble onto the solution. Curiouser and curiouser. Someday, I'd like to meet this fairy mentor of yours. But sure, if she can do potions, have a go. If she manages to replicate it, you'll make someone I know and care about very, very happy.'

Greta beamed as Granny went to put on her best skirt for a night at The Duchess.

26. There Be Dragons

Henry

Early the next day, Henry woke to find leftovers from the grand night at The Duchess and a letter from Greta that she'd gone to see the Blue Fairy about a potion. Henry took one look out of the window, saw a familiar snout and was out the door, grabbing as much of his breakfast as his hands could hold and stuffing bread into his pockets.

The duo was well on their way to Granny's when a shadow fell over the forest.

The boy grabbed the wolf's mane. 'Listen.'

Whoosh.

The wolf perked up her ears and kept walking.

'I think it's a bird,' the boy said. 'Wings make sounds like these.'

Whoosh-whoosh.

Whoosh-whoosh.

WHOOSH-WHOOSH.

'A pretty big bird,' Red told his wolf, looking up at the darkened skies.

Whoosh-whoosh.

Whoosh.

The sun returned from exile.

'I think it flew away,' Henry said, spotting Granny's hut through the thinning trees.

Just as they reached the clearing, darkness descended along with a scaled beast Henry had only seen in fairytale books. In slow motion, first came the tail that swiped a few firtree-tops clean off. Then came two giant clawed legs with a turquoise underbelly and then an eyeball the size of the boy zoomed into view.

THUD.

A purple armored snout exhaled, blowing away half the underbrush.

Henry held onto his wolf as the dust settled.

The beast folded its leathery wings and the sun dared peek out again.

'Um...hello?' Henry said, stepping closer to inspect the creature's glittering scales.

'Hell-oooo,' echoed the beast, lowering its head to sniff the boy.

'Helllll......oooooooooo,' said the second head, approaching Red from his left.

'Hiya,' said the third, bumping heads with the second.

The wolf growled and snapped at the third head, which was too close for comfort.

'Oi, watch it!' the third head said and drew away, hovering above the tree-tops.

'Nooooowwww... Loooook... Whaaaat... Youuuuuu... Diiiiiid... It will sulk for days,' the first head told them.

'Wow. I've only ever seen dragons in picture books,' the boy said. 'Never a real one. I'm Henry, but you can call me Red. Everyone else does.'

'We know.' The first and second heads nodded.

'You do?' Red looked surprised. 'How?'

'We hear her.' The middle head motioned toward the wolf. 'She calls you Henry.'

'We weren't yelling that much in the woods. We know better.' Henry patted his wolf, who pressed her side into the boy's legs.

'We hear her thoughts.'

The boy nodded. 'You are like Ella then. She can hear what people are thinking, too.'

The right head turned toward the middle one. 'Magic returns.'

The two heads nodded and there was a modicum of movement from the third head.

'Princess. Can read minds. We can speak in this Kingdom. Again.'

'What do you mean "again"? You couldn't before?' Red asked. The second head shook vigorously from side to side.

'When she arrived,' the first head motioned at the wolf, 'we lost speech. We got it back when we flew over the mountains. Away. To other kingdoms.'

'Is that where you have been staying?'

Both heads nodded.

'Why did you come back?' the boy asked.

'We sense magic. It pulls us in. We flew over the forest. We sensed it. We landed. You appeared. With her.'

The third head sneaked back down from the tree-tops.

'She is enchanted,' Red said, making the wolf look up.

All three heads nodded. 'We can see,' said the middle one.

'You can sense she isn't really a wolf?' Henry looked surprised.

The middle head nodded. 'When you believe, you can see.'

'And when you believe, you can speak,' said Grizelda, appearing from behind the left head and swatting at it with a tea-towel. 'Hello, Red. As for you, mister dragon, stop blaming the wolf for your misfortunes. Whyever do you think she caused your muteness?'

The third head turned toward Grizelda. 'We felt magic decrease when she appeared. She does not believe.'

'Not. All. Do,' barked Grace.

Red clapped in delight. 'I knew you could speak!'

'Isn't it poetic justice that the one who evicted the dragons,' Grizelda nodded at the wolf, 'also produced the antidote.' She motioned to Henry who looked confused. 'Although, did you have to summon a three-headed dragon as the first one to come back, Red?' She *tsk-tsk*-ed. 'You could have started off with a one-headed dragon, you know.'

Henry looked sheepish. 'I didn't summon anyone. They sensed me.'

'I suppose it could have been worse. You could have summoned a twelve-headed one,' Grizelda relented, patting the dragon's flank.

'Our cousin. We can call to him, if you like?' the left head offered.

'If we think of the map location, he will see it and he can be here in...' the middle head paused, calculating, '...ten minutes.'

The left head nodded a bit too vigorously, making nearby pines billow in the wind as if they were flowers. 'His eighth head has been going bonkers, carrying on and on about coming back for the treasure he left behind, because you see, he hid things good and doesn't want to tell those who can help where to find his secret stash...'

'Gods, no! Not the twelve-headed dragon, no,' Grizelda said. 'You barely fit this meadow. Where will it land? Besides, my house is made of wood and the chances of one out of twelve heads coughing and burning the forest down

- with me and my house in it - are much greater than the chances of one of your three heads coughing. Don't cough!' Grizelda waved her bony finger at the dragon.

None of them saw the tawny wolf hiding in the underbrush, taking turns to snarl at each of the dragon heads, the witch and the black wolf, its eyes trained on the boy in the red T-shirt. The wolf growled impotently once more and slunk back into the forest.

27. The Hut

Henry

At dusk, after dispatching the dragon back to where it had come from, Red and Granny stood in front of her dilapidated hut as if assessing whether it should be allowed to remain standing.

'If Greta is learning potions, I might as well teach you the magic I know. It might come in handy when I'm gone. I can leave you my hut and everything that's in it. You're best suited to hobnob with the dragons and other beasts anyway.'

Henry looked up at her. 'Granny? You are not going anywhere, are you?'

'Not for a few years, I'm not. But we're all mortal. Eventually,' she said and mumbled, 'One would hope. Although with Fate's shenanigans, I'm not so sure what's in store for me.'

'I'm sure fate will be kind to you,' Henry said in earnest, earning a snort from Granny.

'You would think so, wouldn't you? Now, remember the magic words that I taught you?' the woman asked and the boy nodded. 'Say them! Until you learn to whistle like me, you have to say the magic words.'

Henry went up to the hut and stroked one of the logs. '*Eez-bush-ka, eez-bush-ka, vstan k le-su pe-re-dom, ko mne zaa-dom!*' the boy said.

Nothing happened.

'Did I say it wrong?'

'No, no. You said everything right. Hut, oh, hut, stand with your front to the forest and with your back to me. It's just that it's not me saying it, she needs time to adjust,' Granny said.

'You talk about the hut like it's alive,' Red wondered.

The witch coughed to mask a laugh. 'Ha, what do you think, inanimate objects have no soul? Well, this one does. She's been around me long enough to imbibe some sass, too. *Davai-davai*!' She patted one of the logs as if she was patting a horse's rump.

The hut creaked, groaned and grumbled. The earth shook and Henry took a step back. The entire structure rose up a few inches as the hut quacked. Something inside fell and smashed.

'Darn, I forgot to put the water jug away,' mumbled the witch.

The hut rose some more until it towered above them. Slowly, the hut began to turn, stretching its giant chicken legs, one at a time and wriggling its toes while at it. When it was done turning, they found they were facing the back porch with its swing while the front door was now turned toward the forest behind it.

A rope ladder unfurled toward them.

'This is new,' the witch mumbled. 'I think it's for you, Red,' she told him. 'I'm not going to climb that.'

'How are you going to get up there, Granny?' Henry asked, eyeing the hut, still towering above their heads.

'Like this,' the witch said, stretched her arm out and patted one of the logs. '*Saa-dis, sta-rush-ka*. Sit down, you old thing.'

The hut stepped from one leg to another, gathering them up.

Next, the hut sat down with an *oomph*, blowing out a gust of wind from underneath it.

When they were done coughing, Grizelda said, 'Next time, remember not to stand so close, unless you want a bath afterward.'

Henry nodded. 'Okay, Granny. Why did you turn the front door away from us, toward the forest and the back porch to the visitors? Shouldn't it be the other way round?'

'Well, that would depend on where I'm expecting visitors from, don't it?' The witch chuckled and went inside with Henry in tow. 'Today I'm expecting a visitor from the woods. In fact, you know her very well.'

'I do?' The boy eyed the older woman with excitement. 'Who is it?'

'It's your wolf.'

28. Turncoat

At the hut

'My wolf?' Red looked puzzled. 'But we just saw her today, remember? I thought she didn't come into houses. She's never come into Papa's house.'

'Maybe she will someday, now that Papa knows her better,' the witch said.

'He met her?' Henry looked worried. 'Oh, I hope he didn't do anything to her.'

The old woman smiled and ruffled his hair. 'No, he would never do anything to harm her.'

'But he hunts wolves,' Henry said. 'He knows not to hunt her.'

'Really?'

'Really.'

'How do they know each other?' Henry asked.

'She's what you would call a turncoat.' The witch mulled the word over. 'Yes. That's the best way to explain it.'

'What's a turncoat?' Red asked.

'Usually, it is someone who betrays someone else, but that's not your mo...wolf. Your wolf can just turn her coat inside out and be someone else.'

'You mean like magic?' Henry beamed.

'Exactly like magic.'

'Can my wolf turn into anyone I like?' The boy asked.

The witch shook her head.

'No, darling. She only turns into one person.'

'Is she cursed? Like the twelve brothers who were turned into swans by the witch? Like King Thomas was cursed before Queen Belle unenchanted him?' Henry asked.

The woman nodded. 'You could say that.'

'So, my wolf was human before she was a wolf?'

'Yes.'

'And you said it's someone I know very well... Someone Papa knows, too...' Henry furrowed his brow. 'Is it Auntie Mellie? I haven't seen her in a while.'

'No, it's not Mellie,' Granny said. 'I'll let her show you herself. I think I hear her scratching at the door.'

The boy saw two huge green eyes glow from where the back door was ajar.

'She's very brave coming into your hut like that,' Henry whispered.

'She knows nobody intends her any harm here.'

The old woman stood up, uncorked a purple vial and poured out a spoonful. 'Open wide,' she told the wolf. To Henry she said, 'You might want to close your eyes, darling. Your...wolf turning her coat inside out is not a pretty sight.'

The wolf barked and almost ate the spoon.

Henry squished his eyes shut.

'Easy,' the witch told Grace. To the boy she said, 'You might want to close your ears as well, Red.'

Henry did as he was told as the animal went through the cracks and crunches of its metamorphosis.

Grizelda covered the naked panting human form with a blanket.

'Thank you,' came a voice from under the blanket.

'Go put some clothes on.'

The boy's eyes flew open. 'Who is it?'

'Not it, baby. She. Who is she.' The woman rasped, gathering the blanket about her.

'Mama?' The boy hesitated for only a second. 'Mama! Mama! Mama!' He flew at the woman kneeling on the floor with such force that he almost bowled her over.

Grace laughed. 'Easy, baby.'

The boy put his cheek to hers and held her tight around the neck. 'You came back.'

'I never left, baby. I watched over you this whole time,' Grace said into his neck, inhaling the familiar scent.

'I know,' he said and squeezed her harder.

'Easy, baby. I'm here. Mama's here.' Grace started rocking the boy back and forth, ignoring the blanket that was slipping off her shoulder. When she started to hum a lullaby, the boy relaxed and let himself be cuddled in her lap.

'Come, boy, have some sweet tea and let your Mama get dressed or else she's going to catch a cold.' The old woman took the boy's small hand in hers and led him to the table. 'You've had quite a lot of excitement. Sweet tea will help. Here, take a sip.'

Grace retreated into the witch's bedroom never taking her eyes off her son, who by the third sip of his tea, was smiling.

Five minutes later they were all seated at the table as if they always had been.

'Are you going to come back to us now?' Henry asked.

Grace shook her head. 'I can't, baby. I'm a wolf. Granny just lets me turn human every once in a while, with that potion of hers.'

'But you can turn human any time you want?' Henry asked.

'Yes and no. See that bottle?' Grace pointed at the half-empty container. 'We have what we have and when it's gone, it's gone.'

'Besides, it's very painful,' Granny said.

'Painful?' The boy's eyes were as wide as saucers.

Grace smiled and ruffled his hair. 'Don't you worry about that, baby. Don't you worry about any of it one little bit.'

29. The Reunion

Peter

'I'm here! Send him out! I want to get going!' Peter hollered from outside the witch's hut.

Three cups paused mid-air as the trio exchanged looks. Grace put her cup down and went to open the door.

When Peter saw Grace standing in Grizelda's doorway, her shape recognizable in the darkness, in stark contrast against the mellow light coming from inside the hut, his breath caught. He still couldn't get used to seeing Grace in her human form. Holding her gaze, he let his feet guide him toward his wife.

When they were level with each other, Grace smiled, cupped his cheek and said, 'Come in, darling. Would you like some tea?' She took the rifle from his shoulder and deposited it next to the door.

'Papa, look who's here!' Henry beamed as a stunned huntsman loomed in the door frame.

'You...you showed him?' Peter asked and stepped inside, closing the door on a full moon behind him. 'But why?'

Grace shrugged. 'He deserved to know. I deserved a bit of time with my son.' She cuddled Henry close. 'And now I don't have to hide anymore. So, now he knows that I'm the black wolf. It might do him some good, to be able to tell the difference between goodies and bad- dies, seeing how there is a rogue on the loose.'

Henry jumped up and pulled Grace and Peter into a hug. 'Group hug!'

Grace laughed and Granny sniffled. The table cloth created a box of tissues for her, but she hissed at it and the box disappeared.

When Peter released his hold, the boy pulled Grace back to the bench and crawled back into her lap, clutching her neck. 'Mama, I would never have started avoiding the black wolf on account of the tawny one scaring me. I always knew the black wolf was good.'

Granny poured Peter a cup of tea, whispered something to the table cloth and cinnamon rolls appeared.

Henry grabbed for the nearest roll, stuffing his mouth, looking happy as a clam.

'Yes, but I need to teach you that you can trust the pack. The tawny one that scared you is rogue. It doesn't belong here. I don't know where it came from and I'm surprised it hasn't left or tried something,' Grace said.

'Oh, it has tried something, alright.' Peter looked grim. 'Remember what...who we found in the trap by the wheat-field?'

Grace gasped. 'You think... You think *that* was the rogue?'

Peter nodded. 'And the sheep a few weeks ago. Beast thinks it's up to no good.'

Grace's mouth drew into a thin line. 'Then I need to warn them.'

'We.'

'No. The wolves are solitary creatures even if they do unite as packs,' Grace said. 'They are unaccustomed to humans. Besides, how do you envisage doing the talking? Flip charts? Pantomime?'

Henry fidgeted in Grace's lap.

'Have another cinnamon roll and come sit with me while the grown-ups talk,' Granny said and took the boy by the hand. Obediently he jumped down and walked over to the other side of the table.

Peter put his rifle down near the entrance and ruffled his hair. 'I don't know. How do you talk to wolves? With you, I just talked at you.'

'And she can talk back. Can't you, Mama?' Henry interrupted.

'I can, baby, but that's in human speak. With wolves, I'll have to think of something else. Before the rogue does something drastic.'

'It hasn't yet,' Peter said.

'It almost ate Henry!' Granny protested.

'Luckily, it didn't.'

'Luckily my bee-hind,' mumbled Granny. 'If I hadn't taught Red what to do and what not to do...'

Grace squeezed her arm. 'Thank you, Grizelda.'

Peter gave her a curt nod and Granny *huffed*. Undeterred, Peter continued. 'If slaying the sheep and trying to attack a human child count as practice runs, the rogue may be gearing up for something bigger. Like a takeover of the pack.'

'Then we have no time to waste!' Grace said, jumping up. 'I'm about to shift anyway. I could run and...'

Before she could finish the sentence, they heard a bone-piercing howl.

30. Wolfsong

Grace

The howl stretched to the full moon and back, echoing over the hushed woods. Children in the nearby village stilled. Grown-ups quieted. A single note was held to perfection and picked up by one other mourner to give the first one a breather. A new, lower voice joined the lament as the moon watched on. The forest gave up no other sound but the wolfsong. Grace had heard these fateful cries only a few times in the past two years. Whenever the wolves mourned one of their own.

There was a bark and the single note crescendoed in a multitude of howls as the clouds moved in. When the moon was but a sliver of light, only one distant voice remained. And with darkness came silence.

'What was that, Papa? Why are the wolves crying?' Henry asked when he saw Peter gathering up his satchel.

Grace retreated into Granny's bedroom.

'A wolf died tonight, son. The wolfsong is how the pack mourns their dead.'

'They also howl when they are happy, don't they?' Henry asked.

Peter crouched down to his son's height. 'Yes, Henry. They howl to tell rival packs to stay out of their hunting grounds. They howl when they mate. They even howl as a group before the hunt to get a better feeling for the pack. But tonight, something bad has happened.'

'So, when the wolves howl in a group, that's them singing?'

'Yes, it's called wolfsong. Tonight, they are mourning. Lock the door. Don't come out. I'll be back before you know it,' Peter said and headed out the door, grabbing his rifle as he went.

Nobody but the moon saw Grace jump out of the witch's bedroom window in her wolf form.

She ran as fast as her four paws could carry her to be met by a sight she'd seen once in an Earthen storybook. Under the full moon, in the meadow by the caves, a white wolf lay motionless with a black collar under its maw. No, not black. Crimson. Save for the female, the entire pack lay on their stomachs, snouts aimed at the corpse. The widow licked at her mate's ear and emitted a lone howl. The other wolves picked it up.

Grace howled once and turned back, having seen enough.

Half an hour later, Grace stepped out of the shadows and into Peter's path. The moon gleamed above them in the now quiet forest.

'Who was it?' Peter asked.

'Al-pha,' barked the black wolf, her green eyes glowing.

'Which means what?'

'We. Kill. Rogue.'

31. The Killing Kind

Grace

Peter and Grace trekked to the edge of the forest, right to the caves. At the entrance, on a rock shoulder, the rogue stood tall, making itself visible to the pack in the bright moonlight. Behind him, the young female paced to and fro.

As the brown wolf leaped down the ledge and started toward the alpha female of the pack, Grace growled, stepping forward with Peter in tow.

The outsider turned its head and eyed its black nemesis.

The rogue growled once and trotted at Grace, turning its back to the pack. It stopped ten feet from Grace and bared its teeth.

Grace issued a sequence of barks and howls. To Peter she said, 'Told. Them. Who. Did. It.'

The alpha female stood up, her hackles rising. The wolves leapt to their feet and fanned out, encircling the tawny outsider.

The young female stopped pacing, took one last longing look at her suitor and joined her family.

The russet wolf twirled around. Noticing that the young wolves had formed an arc behind him, closing ranks, it snarled at them.

The wolves spread out to form a circle with Grace and Peter completing the formation.

The pack had boxed him in. And accepted that Peter and Grace were there to help.

In an attempt to break through, the intruder launched himself at one of the younger wolves, but had to retreat, shaking his intended victim's elder brother off its mane.

The rogue's eyes darted back and forth as it kept turning around and around.

The villain was surrounded.

The intruder retreated on it hunches and took the only chance left.

It vaulted at the huntsman, teeth bared, the whites of its eyes showing.

Peter's rifle dropped to the ground as the rogue's teeth clasped around his wrist.

'No!' Grace growled and bit down on the rogue's hind leg.

The rogue released Peter and snapped at Grace who had dared to foil his escape.

Grace let go and backed up toward the center of the meadow, drawing the wolf away from Peter.

Without even gracing the human with another look, the russet wolf trod after her, its head held low.

Grace and the interloper circled each other.

The tawny one leaped at her and Grace stuck at it with her front paws.

Then it was Grace's turn to snap at the rogue's neck.

The dance continued as the wolves and the human watched.

The rogue leaned down on its front paws, as if inviting Grace to play.

She growled.

It crept closer, still in its lower-than-thou pose.

Grace stood her ground and glanced at the alpha female, who barked.

The rogue crept even closer.

With their noses almost touching, Grace briefly thought how this must look from the sidelines. *If this wasn't a fight, we might look like two wolves kissing. Except, when you look closer, my teeth are bared and the hackles on the necks of both of us are standing on edge.*

As Grace cast another glance at the alpha female for confirmation about what to do with the intruder, the brown wolf lunged and sank his teeth into her exposed neck, chomping down on her windpipe.

Grace felt herself dragged to the ground, her head hitting the grass with a *thunk.*

The last thing she saw before her eyes fell back into her skull was Peter running at her. That and the alpha female and the pack trampling the rogue.

The moon shone brightly in the drops of blood on the mangled meadow grass.

32. The Agency

Grace

'Oh, hello, Grace,' a Goth-clad pixie said, her eyes briefly straying to Grace from the sixteen TV screens in front of her where more or less horrible things were happening to more or less human beings. 'Aneurysm got you again?'

'Nope,' Grace choked out and took the longest inhale of her life, clawing at her neck. It was smooth and intact. She could breathe again. 'Turns out someone ripping your throat out is exactly as painful as it sounds. This time, I died fighting a rogue wolf. But he got what was coming to him. Glad the Agency hauled me back and resurrected me again,' Grace said, noticing her biking outfit, the one she had been wearing when she had first appeared at the Agency. Eons ago.

'Nobody made you come here in the first place. You clung to Gabriel when he was returning here - after he had just saved you from yet another assassination attempt. The Agency seems to have a mind of its own, because it saved your particulars way back when. So, you will be eternally twenty-five when you get back here. And...you know better than anyone that...' Loretta searched for something, never lifting her gaze from one screen, 'the only way you usually end up here is...'

'When I die. I know, I know. Once imprinted, always imprinted in the form I had when I first came here, right?'

'You have complaints, you take it up with you know who.' Loretta pointed her thumb upstairs.

'No thanks. I'm okay losing fifteen years or more every time I die.'

'That's not all you lose. Feel the effects yet?' Loretta asked.

Grace exhaled. 'I should be more agitated, considering I died, shouldn't I?'

'Yup. Feel the peace and eternal natural bliss spreading through your veins with every breath you take?'

'I should be kicking and screaming, trying to get back to Peter and Henry, shouldn't I?' Grace mused, towering behind Loretta, feeling eerily calm. She always felt calm at the Agency of Guardian Angels.

'Come on, come on, she has already left for church, when does she drop the book?' Loretta mumbled.

'Hey, that fairy is not in peril,' Grace said, casting curious glances at Loretta. 'And she looks a little familiar...'

'Someone is about to drop a book on that fairy's head from the quarters above and detain her and ruin her life. Or not, as it may turn out,' the pixie said, biting her nails. 'Where the hell is she?'

'She? Loretta, are you sure someone is in the quarters above?'

On-screen, the fairy was already at the window, testing her wings as if she was just getting used to them.

With the joystick Loretta zoomed into the tulip above the one the girl was occupying.

'It's empty! Where is Morgana?' Loretta growled.

'Morgana? As in Fairy Queen Morgana?' Grace asked.

'She's supposed to drop a book...that book,' the pixie pointed to the shelf behind her, 'on that fairy's head who will then curl up on that chair and start reading it.'

The fairy on the screen flitted to stand on the window-sill and surveyed the room as if she was trying to memorize everything.

Grace looked at the blond fairy on the screen and then at the raven-haired pixie with her purple streaks in front of her.

'That's you, isn't it?' Grace asked. 'Not your twin sister?'

The pixie nodded and punched a red button on her desk. All sixteen screens froze and the fairy they were watching paused mid-flight off the ledge.

Grace picked up the hefty volume from the shelf and handed it to Loretta. 'I think you need to throw it at yourself, honey. Nobody else is coming. So, if you want your life to turn out just like it already did...'

The pixie took the book.

'Except I don't understand, how come you are seeing yourself in the past?' Grace asked.

Loretta shrugged. 'It's Magic Kingdom. It exists outside of Time, floating betwixt past and present, never staying too long anywhere. Just surfacing every once in a while, to remind people of the fairytales long forgotten. I was transported there on the eve of my sixteenth birthday and was *en route* to repeat Andersen's Thumbelina tale. Except I missed my wedding because I read this book for two hours straight.'

The pixie stroked the leather-bound volume as if it was her most prized possession and then threw the book at the screen. It hit the fairy in the back and Time restarted. The blond girl caught the book before it toppled to the ground and returned to inspect it. As she flipped the book open, Grace recognized the hunger she had seen dozens of times in the pixie's eyes when she was on to something intriguing.

Loretta *phew*-d and sprawled across her chair, the other screens still temporarily frozen.

The pixie leaned forward and grabbed the joystick, zooming in. 'Just to make sure Edwin's life also turns out the way it should...' She zoomed in on the church and the fairy prince pacing the pavement in front of it.

'Where's the new girl?' Loretta mumbled. 'Is nothing going according to plan?' She spied Morgana who was about to fly off. 'Oh, no, you don't. You're not going back to get me, thank you very much!'

Out of thin air, a willowy spirit materialized behind Loretta's chair.

'Where...where am I?' A girl with eyes the size of saucers wafted above them. 'Is this the afterlife?' she asked and noticed the fairy prince on-screen. 'Oh, he's charming, isn't he?'

Loretta eyed Morgana and the prince and the spirit again. 'Fine, I'll have to do everything myself! Hello, dear. How would you like to be a princess in your afterlife?'

'Me, a princess?' The girl brought her translucent hands together. 'But I'm a poor match girl, I'm not...'

'It's the afterlife. Have you been a good girl?' Loretta asked the spirit and winked at Grace.

The girl nodded just as Morgana was extending her wings, ready to take flight.

'Freeze her,' Loretta said.

Grace punched the red button.

'Well, good girls deserve do-overs,' the pixie said and pointed at the screen. 'Do you want to live happily ever after as a fairy in a magic flower colony and marry a prince? Your mother-in-law is a bit scary, but I wouldn't worry about her for too long.'

'Better to have a mother figure than no mother at all,' the Match Girl said.

Loretta had to agree. 'My mother died when I was born.'

'Time won't stay frozen forever, girls,' Grace reminded them.

'Right. Do you want to live there?' Loretta zoomed out and showed the fields of flowers of the colors of the rainbow.

The Match Girl gasped. 'Oh, my….'

'There. With the fairies. Be their princess?' The pixie got a nod out of the recently departed Match Girl.

'Alright then. In you go.' The pixie gestured at the screen. 'Except, wait a minute…' Loretta snapped her fingers and the girl's body turned solid and sprouted giant pink wings from her back.

'Just let the prince do all the talking, okay? Now go!'

The Match Girl touched the surface and the screen sucked her in, shrinking her to thimble-size. A second later, she knocked over the fairy prince who didn't seem to mind.

'That went well. I think,' the pixie threw her feet clad in Doc Martens onto the table. 'I think hot chocolates are in order. Fetch us some, will ya?'

Grace walked over to a dispenser in an alcove and wished for hot chocolate. Twice. She returned with two steaming cups.

'Thank you!' said the pixie. 'Now what should we do with you this time around?'

Grace held up her hands. 'There is no 'this time'. It's still the 'last time'. I'm not finished. Send me back.'

'Send you back? What do you think Gabriel will have to say about that?'

'I don't care. He changed me into a wolf and reinserted me into the fairytale as a horrible warning. As if being a wicked stepmother to Ella for three years wasn't enough. Still, I'd like to continue being that horrible warning, if you please,' Grace said.

'You love him that much?' A blond hunk of a man appeared in the doorway, folding his immense iridescent wings.

'Them, Gabriel. Them,' Grace said. 'Peter and Henry. And yes, I do. And it's not going to change.'

Gabriel looked Grace in the eye. She stood her ground and she knew how it must look. A giant of a man towering over a tiny smidgen of a girl in biking gear that barely came up to his chest. Fifteen years ago, he had stepped in front of a bus for her. She wasn't angling for a fight, but she would fight, if she had to.

I will always keep fighting to go back to them.

I know.

At the Agency, having private telepathic chats was easiest. If they wanted others to stay out of things.

Then why don't you help me? Let me be me. With them. Human. Why do I have to be a wolf? Marina's...Grizelda's potion is running out. Please.

Gabriel sighed.

Loretta felt the need to turn around to observe their silent exchange. 'Are you having a conversation without me?'

Gabriel smiled at both of them.

I will let you go on one condition.

Name it.

You will remain in the Magic Kingdom for another fifteen years and help Henry rebuild the fairytales...

Deal!

I wasn't finished. And if you die, you will be resurrected and then reinserted...

Deal!

I wasn't finished. You will turn back into your twenty-five-year-old self when that happens – as you have until now. Peter might be fifty-five. Henry might be twenty. If you die...when you die...whenever you die, you will always be reinserted into the Magic Kingdom in your twenty-five-year-old body.

I think Peter can get away with taking a new *lover every once in a while. His paramours will just keep getting younger and younger. I can change my hair and clothes a bit every time I go back. And my name. There are variations of Grace we could use - Greylyn, Graciela, Grazia... It is not uncommon for men to go after a certain type of woman, so I don't think I would have to change that much. I think we could handle it.*

Gabriel nodded once. 'Then consider this a very protracted save in the Magic Kingdom to bring it back to life.'

'A save? Would I have to accept being a guardian angel for the Agency?'

'Not if you don't want to. The Agency has already accepted you and started resurrecting you every time you end up here. It already considers you a guardian. Whether you say yes or no, it's immaterial.'

'Still, I'd rather not say yes yet. I can be a guardian of magic, like you said I would be when we met on Earth.'

'Back in the day, you did say she would have an impact on magic across dimensions,' Loretta mused, still glued to her screens.

'Maybe that's what I was meant to do all along? Be in Magic Kingdom? Not just guard a few Goddesses who were reclaiming their magic powers on Earth,' Grace said.

Gabriel shrugged. 'A guardian of magic is simply someone who can run a marathon rather than a sprint. Or write a novel rather than an article.'

The pixie chuckled. 'I'd say yes quickly if I were you while he is in a good mood, Grace.'

'Yes. I accept.' Grace said. 'Being the guardian of magic, not a guardian angel. But I will have a think about that, too.'

'In that case, make a wish,' Gabriel said.

'A wish?' Grace asked, remembering Grizelda's warnings. 'Like - I wish I was no longer a wolf and that I was returned back to my family? That kind of wish?'

Gabriel inclined his head. 'I've been told that all it takes to break that curse is for you to wish for it. And you just did.'

'You've been told? By whom? Did Grace's wish just undo her wolf-curse or something?' Loretta asked with her back to them, having long turned back to the screens.

'Yes.'

'I really was cursed?' Grace asked, trying to feel surprised and failing.

'Does you being turned into a beast for failing to uphold your end of the bargain remind you of something?' the angel asked.

'Beast...Tom was turned into an animal for being rude to a fairy. But that curse was cast by Morgana. As was the counter curse Belle mistakenly used as a cure. Was this...my curse Morgana's doing as well?' Grace asked, trying to get upset and failing. Her heart beat slow and steady and it was as if adrenalin had been switched off permanently in her system.

'Yes,' Gabriel admitted.

'Really? How did you cast it? Did you have to say anything? Do anything?' Loretta hit the red button and froze Time. 'Do tell.'

'Like you, I simply had to make a wish,' Gabriel told Grace.

'Okay gotcha, gotta be careful with those wishes. Anything else?' The pixie had flipped out a pad, reached for a pencil behind her ear and was taking notes.

Grace rolled her eyes. 'You wished for me to turn into a wolf? Great! Thank you! Now that it's over, if you don't mind, as much as I like the Agency-imposed Xanaxed-out tranquility, it dulls my senses. So, can I please go back to my family?' Grace begged.

'If you want to get back, jump.' Gabriel motioned at the screen showing a nook of the forest in front of a familiar hut.

'You're really letting me go?' Grace asked and looked up into the big hunk's eyes, finding a clear resolve in his marble features. 'Thank you!' She stood up on tiptoes, but reconsidered hugging him.

'If you go now, maybe nobody will notice you were gone?' The pixie put in her tuppence.

'I doubt Peter and the wolves missed the fact that the rogue chomped down on my windpipe and I disappeared,' Grace said wryly, but jumped into the screen nevertheless.

'WOW.' THE PIXIE SWIVELED her chair to face her boss. 'Your face. It's completely blank. You're never going to tell her, are you?' she demanded.

'Tell her what? There is nothing of consequence to tell. I made Peter go into the cafe where Grace worked. They met. The rest is history,' Gabriel said.

'Could you be any less human?' The pixie huffed.

'Angel, remember?' Gabriel said.

'You weren't always.'

'That was nine hundred years ago.' A shadow that looked a lot like regret passed over his chiseled features.

'No, that was sixteen Earth and thirty-two Agency years ago. Not that long. You saved her. You made a deal with the Boss so he wouldn't just harvest her as a guardian at the tender age of twenty-five. You fell in love with her. Where is all of that now?' Loretta asked.

The angel smiled without any warmth reaching his eyes and evaporated in a cocoon of white light.

33. The Royals

Grace

Hopping through the screen, Grace landed in the outskirts of the meadow next to Granny's hut. The clearing had seen better days. What grass remained was singed, a few trees around the perimeter had been snapped in two and there was a funny-shaped dent in the middle. Hearing voices, she retreated behind a birch tree and crouched in the ferns.

'Did I say anything when I had to explain to Henry that his Mama had gone away for a while when Grace disappeared two weeks ago? No!' It sounded like Grizelda.

Two weeks? She hadn't been at the Agency even an hour. Time did move in mysterious ways in the Magic Kingdom.

Grace hazarded a peek, curious as to who Granny Grizelda was lecturing. She spotted a shape, but the man's back was to the forest, so she couldn't tell who he was. The thought of seeing Grizelda again brought a smile to her face. She couldn't wait to tell her...

Grace's thoughts were interrupted by Grizelda's continuing tirade.

'Did I say anything when all of you started coming round my hut at any time of day and night? No!' Grizelda stomped about on her porch, the floor boards, creaking. 'But you cannot just camp out here. Go home! To Henry! I am up to the wazoo with dragons...'

Home to Henry? Peter! Grizelda is talking to Peter!

What will he do when he sees me, all human again? What will he say?

Butterflies fluttered in the pits of her stomach and Grace felt her cheeks blush, her agency-administered calm gone. As she felt her humanity returning Grace stood up and stepped out from behind the tree.

'You!' Came a shout across the meadow. 'How are you even alive?' Grizelda yelled. 'Peter saw you die! He had to tell Henry...' the old woman babbled.

'Hello.' Grace waved at them, feeling her blush reach her nose as Peter rushed over and pulled her into an embrace.

'You're back!' Peter whispered and stroked her short hair. 'And you're you...'

'You knew this would happen, didn't you?' Grizelda's hands went to her hips as she leaped across the clearing, staring at the both of them. 'Why didn't you tell me?'

'I didn't know I'd be back,' Grace said.

'You're telling me the mean angels could have not let you go?' Grizelda looked aghast.

Peter and Grace both nodded.

'Okay we go in and then you tell me about how they let you come back as a human,' the older woman decided and headed back to her hut.

Half an hour later, just when Grace had almost finished telling Peter the good news that she was no longer cursed to roam the woods on four paws, a royal delegation - King Thomas, Queen Belle, Ella and Prince Nicholas - tumbled out of the mirror and into the hut.

'Hey, who invited you?' Granny narrowed her eyes at the newcomers.

'Apologies, Granny,' the king said. 'I thought I saw someone who looked an awful lot like Grace through the mirror...'

'And I told him no, it's Grizelda's apprentice,' Belle said.

'And I still vouched it was Grace and we listened in and realized it *was* Grace, so we told Ella and Nick and decided to pop over,' King Thomas finished.

'You saw Grace through my mirror?!?' The old woman hissed. 'Have you been spying on me all along?'

'Don't worry, Granny, King Thomas didn't always know your mirror is a gateway,' Ella said.

The king forced a smile. 'I only found out recently about your looking-glass being a portal, Grizelda.'

'And I found out about the dragons,' Ella piped up. 'They are going to teach me how to use my gift better.'

Grace blinked. 'Okay, I die for a while and all of a sudden dragons appear who know telepathy and palace mirrors become portals. Could someone please explain what has happened in those two weeks that I've been gone?' Grace asked as Peter clutched her hand.

'Two weeks? You were gone for two years!' Belle said. 'The last we saw you was before Ella married Nick. Where did you go for two years?'

'It's a long story.' Grace sighed. The royals hadn't seen her since Nick "rescued" Ella from Grace's "evil" clutches and the day after Grace had been turned into a wolf.

'Not that long a story,' Peter said. 'She's a guardian angel. She's been guarding Henry for two years. In wolf form. And before then she was guarding Ella. Posing as a wicked stepmother,' Peter said, taking Grace's hand.

Beast and Ella looked thoughtful, Belle gaped and Nicholas looked interested.

Grace opened her mouth to protest that she hadn't accepted to be a guardian angel, but decided not to muddle the waters. Instead, she explained, 'I got posted here five years ago, two of which I've spent in wolf form. Two weeks ago, I fought a rogue wolf, it got me, I died, was resurrected and sent back as a human this time.'

'I hope you didn't make another bargain,' Peter said, pulling Grace closer.

'Nope. I just asked. Nicely.'

'Bargain? And guarding in wolf form...' Ella said. 'It was you I sensed in the forest a month ago!'

Grace shrugged. 'Could be. I remember hearing your thoughts the day you left for the palace. Maybe your gift has developed and now you can hear me as well?'

'Why two weeks?' Nick asked.

'Technically, I was at the Agency for less than an hour,' Grace said. 'I returned as soon as I could. An hour had passed where I was. Here, two weeks. Time flows differently...at the Agency.' Grace decided to tell a half-truth.

Ella narrowed her eyes at her.

'Now, tell me what's been going on here,' Grace said. 'Where's Henry?'

'He's with Greta at The Duchess,' Peter reassured her. 'We'll go see him later.'

'Or you could talk to Greta and have them pop over here in seconds,' the king suggested.

Grace looked at him. *Have they discovered airplanes or hovercars or teleportation in the two weeks I've been gone? I must have a chat with the Warriors about how much of the modern-day alien contraband they are leaking into this near-medieval society.*

Grace noticed Ella perked up and was about to ask her something, so she quickly issued a question of her own, 'What do you mean, Tom?'

Belle bristled at Grace's frivolous address of the ruling monarch and adjusted her crown.

King Thomas stepped up to Granny's bronze mirror and said, 'Show me the silver mirror.'

The mirror obliged, showing an archway, beyond which lay the kitchen, where Henry was playing with pots and pans and Greta was stirring something in a pot. Or rather, the wooden spoon was stirring something in the pot with Greta watching over it.

'Greta, Henry, look who's here!' Tom shoved Grace in front of himself.

'Mama!' The boy ran the few steps it took to cross the hall and leaped through the mirror, never thinking it to be impossible.

Greta followed, hitching up her skirts and looking right and left, but not before she said something to the fire under the pot and it dimmed down.

'Now I understand why when Peter and I still lived in that house I kept finding you in my hallway, Tom, looking like you had no idea how you got there,' Grace said. 'You've been using my hall mirror to go back and forth where precisely?' Grace looked up at the king, while cuddling Henry.

'Sometimes I've been to see the Warriors, other times...other places,' Beast said, looking apologetic. 'I should have told you. But I didn't want to tempt you. Plenty have lost their lives travelling by way of mirrors.'

'Lost their lives? And you travel like that all the time?' Belle asked, her hand flying to her mouth. 'You and I, we are going to talk about this,' Belle said.

Beast mumbled something to the extent that he knew what he was doing.

'At home,' Belle intoned.

'Yes, yes, could you please all go home now,' Grizelda said.

'Granny!' Ella looked mortified and pointed at a wicker basket Prince Nicholas was holding. 'You don't have to worry, we brought food for everyone.'

Belle composed herself, plastered on a wide smile and clapped her hands. 'That's right. Now that Grace has returned, it's time for a little celebration, don't you think?'

'It's not the food I'm worried about,' mumbled Grizelda. 'I'm sorry if I'm not terribly enthusiastic about celebrations or if I don't seem too welcoming.'

'You have your reputation.' Belle offered a soothing smile.

'Of a recluse, yes. But it's not my reputation I'm worried about, it's my sanity. I have patience and it's been worn thin,' snapped the old woman. 'I seem to be getting lots of visitors as of late. Too many, in fact. First, after the three-headed one left, a whole delegation of dragons arrived. There were three beasts, one three-headed, one nine-headed and one twelve-headed, and three of my favorite meadows in this forest will never be the same again, let me tell you. The dragons requested to see the two of you,' Granny pointed at Belle and Ella, 'and offered to tutor Ella in telepathy. They will even allow her to take David along, but Nicholas is dead set against it,' she added for Grace's benefit. 'Then, the Warriors came, or well...just one very large, very beautiful warrior who nearly made me forget the love of my life. He took one look at Hans chopping wood for my stove and recruited him on the spot. Bye-bye, Hans!' Grizelda threw her hands up in the air and hit Beast square in the chest. Instead of an apology, she said, 'You're standing too close and there are too many of you.'

As the king perched himself on the bench, Granny continued. 'At least they all brought useful gifts. Even though the dragons almost incinerated my home and I thought the warrior was going to poke my eye out with his perky nipples every time I turned around. My hut's just too small for big hunks of men or too many people.' Granny growled. 'Now whyever did you lot think that my little dingy hut is the best place to host a party where...' She counted her visitors. 'Not one, but...two, three, four royals are in attendance?' Grizelda's hands flew to her hips.

'Well, we can't have it at the castle now, can we,' Belle said and patted Grizelda's arm, motioning for everyone to take a seat around the long table. 'Everyone there knows Grace from before her...rejuvenation.' She assessed Grace up and down. 'But they might still recognize her. We did.'

'True. Also, everyone at the palace hates Grace,' Nicholas said and raised his hands. 'I don't. Not anymore. Welcome back, Grace!' He stepped up and gave her a tentative hug.

That seemed to wake everyone up. The newcomers descended on Grace as Henry buried his face in her neck.

Grace welcomed the embraces and almost missed a hooded figure in a forest-green cloak stepping out of the mirror.

'Dragons and Warriors should be the least of your problems,' said the newcomer. 'Fairies and pixies without rulers, however...' The figure slipped off her hood, shaking her auburn tresses loose.

34. The Quest

At the hut

'Morgana,' Grace whispered, throwing a glance at Peter and holding Henry close.

Granny eyed the eavesdropping woman in her burgundy dress without offering her a place at their table. 'What is this, everybody come by Mari...Grizelda...Granny's hut day? What are *you* doing here?'

'I have a problem,' Morgana said, smiled tentatively at Peter and sat down stiffly.

Peter slid down the bench and away from her curves.

'I'd say, considering you just walked in unannounced and unwanted. You think I'll help you after what you did to Grace?' Granny spat.

Morgana's eyes flashed green, and Beast who happened to be sitting across from her thought he glimpsed fangs. 'I have no idea what you're talking about. I did nothing but a kindness to Grace. Tell her!' The woman ordered, pointing a finger at Grace.

'Morgana did me the kindness of letting me borrow her body for almost three years so I could care for Henry without keeling over mid-anything when my aneurysm went kaboom,' Grace admitted and thought whether she should add that it was Morgana's curse that had turned her into a wolf.

Grizelda *hunhed* as the royals gaped.

'Doesn't mean everyone liked being duped,' Grizelda said.

Morgana looked at Granny and smiled. 'Oh, you have no idea, darling.'

'Of the extent of your duplicity?' The older woman pouted. 'I can guess, don't you worry. Now you said you had a problem? Out with it then! We were about to have a party here until you so rudely interrupted us.' Granny scowled at Belle and the wicker backset and went to get her magic table cloth.

Morgana shrugged and rolled her eyes at Grace. 'Always such a blunt axe, darling. And you wonder where Mellie gets it from.' When she got nothing back, Morgana primped her auburn locks and relented. 'Very well. After I returned to the Flower Colonies two years ago, after carrying Grace's spirit around for three years before that,' Morgana slid her hands over her body, 'my kingdom was still functioning rather well. My son had done a marvelous job holding things together and that wife of his, while feeling rather poorly, stuck by him like a leaf to a tree. I let them carry on for a couple of more years, just to be sure they were fit to rule and now... Now, he's disappeared and she's dead. And I can't find him! I need Edwin found! Immediately!' Morgana stuck her chin up.

'Maybe you need a detective...erm... huntsman for this job?' Grizelda opined. 'Maybe your son's wife being dead has something to do with why he disappeared?'

'Don't you dare accuse him. He loved her! Well, as much as a fickle fairy can love...' Morgana looked deflated.

Belle handed the Fairy Queen a steaming cup.

'What's this?' Morgana demanded.

'Chamomile tea. You look like you could use some, Godmother,' Belle said and everyone gaped.

'Godmother?' Ella choked out.

Morgana threw them all a smile as she took the proffered cup. 'Fairy Godmother. Fairy Queen. Because somebody has to be.' She took a sip of her tea and declared, 'Edwin couldn't have done it. He left first. Then she died. I think Edwin went to find a cure and just...disappeared. Meanwhile, his wife died of grief. How stupid. They didn't even have any kids. Now I have to stick around until...' Morgana bit her lip.

Grizelda put a hand over the Fairy Queen's and Morgana's other hand froze *en route* to her mouth. 'Tell us everything from the very beginning.'

'The last I heard...'

'From the very beginning...' the old woman repeated.

'Oh, for the love of...' Morgana set her cup down and some tea sloshed out. 'One minute Edwin was there, vowing to find a cure for his dying wife and planning to go see a powerful wizard, and the next thing he's gone and she dies, partly from heart-break and partly from poor health. I mean, I'm amazed she lasted this long with her delicate sensibilities. I have scried for Edwin, I have cast spells to summon him back. Nothing works. It's like he isn't even...'

'...in this dimension anymore.' Grizelda and Morgana both finished in unison.

'Did he say which powerful wizard he was going to see?' Grace asked.

'That's the thing. There are no powerful wizards left in the Magic Kingdom – except for me, of course – but I think Edwin was talking about a male wizard,' Morgana admitted.

'The only male wizard I know – and he isn't really a wizard, he's more of a charlatan – is Mellie's Ozzy or Oz as he calls himself,' Granny mumbled.

'Yes, that's it. Edwin did mention an Oz.'

'Are you sure?' Ella intervened.

Morgana nodded and looked about at everyone as if she was seeing them for the very first time. 'Oh, my. What a turn-out. The entire royal family, minus the munchkin and the reunited family here as well. Hello, Henry,' she said to the boy huddled in Grace's lap.

Henry waved and smiled.

'If it was Oz your boy went to see, then he would have had to go to a different dimension. Oz doesn't live in Magic Kingdom.' Granny said. 'Mellie has been trying to get to him every which way and she hasn't been able to find him. How did Edwin plan to contact him, do you know?'

Morgana inclined her head and turned to inspect the mirror. 'The silly boy knew I used mirrors to travel through worlds.'

Grace glanced at Beast who looked pensive.

'If he knew he had to go to another world, maybe he used a mirror to do it?'

'Whose mirror? I mean, where would he find one? It's not like magic mirrors hang on every wall, you know,' Grace said, looking unsure.

'Where would you fit a magic mirror in your flower colony anyway? In a flower?' Grizelda scoffed and narrowed her eyes at Morgana. 'Care to share how you use mirrors to travel through worlds? I just use mine to show me things.'

'I don't need to have a mirror myself. I just need to know where to find one. You have one.' Morgana nodded at the bronze frame she had emerged from a quarter of an hour before.

'It came with the hut. In the best folklore traditions of my home... mirrors are used to look for things. That's why it's called a looking glass.' Granny said. 'And...'

Morgana put up a hand to spare herself the lecture. 'You,' Morgana nodded at Grace, 'You used to have two mirrors at The Duchess - one golden and a silver one,' Morgana said.

The Beast nodded. 'I usually used the silver one in your hallway.'

'Not that I knew what to do with them,' Grace said through gritted teeth, glaring at Beast.

King Thomas had the decency to look ashamed.

'Are mirrors made from metal?' Henry piped up.

'Henry, darling,' Morgana said and patted him on the head. 'I think it's a marvelous thing that you brought the dragons back, thank you. Well, since you ask, the frames are usually made of metal,' Morgana told him. 'Magic mirrors themselves - only Time knows what they are made of.' Morgana winked at the boy.

'Does anyone have an iron one?' Henry asked.

Morgana and Granny just stared at him.

'Mama had a gold mirror and a silver one, Ella took the golden one,' said Henry.

Belle glanced at Beast and Grace thought on whose orders Ella knew to grab that mirror from her old bedroom and if she could ask for the royal family to give it back.

Meanwhile, Henry carried on, 'The silver one is still at The Duchess and Granny has a bronze one.' He pointed at the mirror in the corner. 'Is there an iron mirror?'

'Iron is not healthy for fairies,' Morgana said, chewing her lip. 'I'm immune, of course, but not Edwin.'

Grace raised an eyebrow as did Granny.

'It's not deadly, exactly, but it repels fairies and binds them in place,' Morgana explained.

'So, what would happen, if a fairy prince travelled from a magic mirror he somehow found, to somewhere there was an iron mirror on the receiving side?' Grace asked.

'He wouldn't get through. But then he would be back and he isn't.'

'Maybe there is an enchantment on that receiving mirror to punish intruders?' Belle asked.

Grizelda mumbled, glancing at her bronze looking glass, 'Now why didn't I think of that before?'

'What if there is such an iron mirror and there is an enchantment on it? What could it do? What would you do?' Morgana looked at Grizelda expectantly.

Grace mumbled, 'Turn him into a frog,' and got The Look from Grizelda.

'Shush. I was within my rights,' Granny retorted. 'Now, if I didn't want any visitors and was in a punishing mood... I would turn him into something nasty or expunge him somewhere unpleasant. Or both.' Granny shrugged.

'So, my son is goddesses knows where.' Morgana looked thoughtful.

Granny narrowed her eyes at the Fairy Queen and whispered to Grace, 'How does she know about goddesses?' The comment earned her a sly look from Morgana.

'If Edwin went to see Oz maybe he is still in Oz?' Ella offered.

'Then one of you must go to Oz,' Morgana proclaimed.

'One of us? Must go? Why not you? Got better things to do than rescue your son?' Granny glared at the Fairy Queen.

Morgana looked straight back at Grizelda and sighed. 'I can't leave Terramara without a ruler. No Edwin, no princess, no queen, what do you think will happen to my fickle fairies? Things will fall apart in my flower colony. I don't know how long this quest will take. Someone else will have to go. Now the question is - who?'

'Nick, you have always complained that you never get to do anything courageous,' Beast clapped his son on the back. 'I think you could do with a quest, what say you?'

'Absolutely not,' Belle proclaimed and Ella nodded.

'But Ella and Nick already have a son, the succession is secure,' Tom said.

'Sure, Ella could be the Vice Regent until David comes of age, should anything happen, but the point is, I don't want anything to happen to *my* only...' Belle parried.

'Our.' Beast interjected.

'Our only son.'

'I could change the curse so you could have more children, if that's what all of this is about,' Morgana said as simply as if she were ordering tea.

Everyone looked at her, sporting long faces.

Granny thought this an opportune moment to whisper something to the table cloth, which started producing delicious delights.

'What? What did I say? I offered a solution.' The Fairy Queen pointed out.

'No, thanks,' Belle retorted. 'I know you and your solutions. I don't trust you and your solutions, *Godmother*.'

'I'd like to go,' Nicholas said, looking thoughtful and earning a horrified squeak from Ella.

'And so, we have a Cowardly Lion...' Morgana mused.

'I'll let you go only if you promise to come back to me,' Ella strengthened her grip on Nick's arm as Belle nodded.

'Listen, Edwin is not dead or in peril. I'm quite sure. Otherwise, all hell would already have broken loose. He is just stuck somewhere and needs retrieving. It's a simple search and rescue mission. In a dimension where the main ruler is ...well, magically inept. Prince Nicholas will never be in harm's way,' Morgana reassured everyone.

'Do you swear?' Belle asked.

'Every damn day,' Morgana parried.

'You know what I meant.'

'I know. And I chose not to answer your question, dear.'

'So, you don't know if those that go on this "search and rescue mission" as you put it will all come back?' Ella asked.

'Those that go? Who besides Nicholas needs to go?' Belle asked.

'Why, Mellie, of course.' Morgana smiled, stood up and reached for an éclair. 'Didn't you say she has been dying to find this Oz?' she asked Grizelda who nodded. 'She's motivated. It will help.'

'You make sure they both come back.' Ella clung to Nicholas.

'It's a quest, not a high-ropes adventure course where everyone makes it out alive.' Morgana smirked, biting down on her confection as she circled the end of the table toward where Ella was sitting.

'Then Nicholas is not going,' Ella said, looking up, her mouth drawn in a thin line.

Morgana smiled and shook her head. 'He doesn't need to go today. Tomorrow is soon enough. You'll both have time to think and argue about whether or not you want more kids.'

Morgana leaned in, her dark auburn tresses spilling over Ella's shoulders and whispered so low only the princess could hear, 'What if something even better than what Fate's got in store for your mother here might befall her there?'

Ella inhaled sharply and turned, her face nose-to-nose with the Fairy Queen's.

Morgana winked. The Fairy Queen sashayed back to where Grace's family was sitting and crouched to Henry's level. 'Henry, dear, care to give a villain her happily ever after?'

Epilogue

After most of the guests had gone and Grizelda was cleaning up, she heard a noise in her bedroom that sounded a lot like yawning. When Grizelda went to have a look, she saw her daughter stretched out on her bed.

'Are they all finally gone?' Mellie asked, ambling up on her elbow.

'What the heck are you doing here?' Grizelda hissed, aware the door was ajar. 'I mean I know why you didn't join us – too much pretending required and you didn't know if you could glamour everyone to like you – but what are you doing here?' Grizelda asked as something clanged in the other room.

'Careful,' Grace told Peter, who was carrying a few plates to Grizelda's kitchen. Grace took the cutlery from Henry. 'Maybe you and Papa could go outside and play while Granny and I finish up here?' She suggested, casting glances at the bedroom.

'Don't be long.' Peter smooched Grace on the cheek and patted her bum, making her blush.

'Soon. I'm home now. We have all the time in the world. I'll be but a moment.' Grace pulled him close and kissed him quick.

'I'd say get a room, but mine is occupied,' Grizelda smirked. 'I'm going, I'm going,' Peter waved at her and left.

Only then did Mellie deign to join them, swiping the last éclair from a plate.

Grizelda grabbed the few remaining cups off the table and handed Mellie the dish cloth.

'What, pray tell, am I to do with that?' Mellie crinkled her nose and held the cloth between two fingers.

'I wash, you dry. It's the least you can do for eavesdropping,' the old woman admonished. 'Were you here the entire time?'

Mellie took the cloth, stuffed the rest of the éclair into her mouth and shrugged. 'I may have heard some things. Then I fell asleep. And woke up when someone said my name. Who was that lady?'

'Oh, you don't know her. And you don't want to know her,' Grizelda said, knowing Mellie would probably sell her soul to ask Morgana for favors.

Mellie gave Grace a once-over. 'Seems that the royal family has taken quite a shine to you. Forgave you your evil ways.'

Grace rolled her eyes. 'It's nice to see you too, Mellie.'

Mellie huffed and sidled up to her mother.

For a while, they labored in silence. Grizelda washed, Mellie dried and Grace kept bringing more things to the kitchen.

'Why did you come? Did you need something?' Grizelda asked Mellie.

'We didn't finish our conversation the other day,' Mellie said, setting down a cup.

'The other day? That was more than two weeks ago!' Grizelda huffed. 'Although I should be grateful that you visit me at all. I guess now it's safe, me being a reformed cannibal and all.' She smirked.

'Mother!'

'Now I'm Mother. At least that's an improvement from "witch",' Grizelda said.

'You're never going to let me forget about it, are you?' Mellie's chin quivered. 'Last time I came by, I wanted to tell you something. I was hoping for sympathy...I thought you as a mother would understand... Instead, I found you were harboring her!' Mellie glared at Grace, 'And I wasn't able to talk to you about me at all!'

Grizelda saw the corners of Mellie's mouth taking a dive and heard the sobs start. She sighed, took the cloth from Mellie and sat her down into the only comfortable chair in the room.

'Tell me.'

'You know, Oz tricked me,' Mellie said, fingering the table cloth. 'He told me if I gave him Ellie, he would wait for me to happily place all the other kids with people they love.'

Grace raised an eyebrow at Grizelda, mouthing 'place?' which Mellie ignored.

'And once I'd placed them, then we could be reunited as a happy family in the Emerald City. He never came to get me!' She wailed, throwing herself onto the table. When her shoulder shakes elicited no sympathy, she raised her head, eyes dry. 'I did get a note, though.'

'A note?'

'That Ellie is in Heaven.' Tears started streaming down Mellie's face, her black mascara running rivulets on her flushed cheeks.

Grace eyed her suspiciously. Mellie was capable of anything. Could she be acting to get her way? For them to tell her how she could reach Oz.

This was Magic Kingdom. Anything was possible.

'So, he took such good care of your baby that she died and for all you know he is still philandering around the dimensions? Did you have to step into the same shit that I did, Melisandra?' Grizelda asked. 'I thought I told you about your cad of a father...' Seeing Mellie's shell-shocked expression Grizelda stopped.

'Oz is not like that! He took to Ellie. I saw him looking at her tiny little face and the way he looked at her, he loved her. LOVED HER!' Mellie yelled. 'And then she DIED!'

'He might have loved her, but wait until she started crying for food and pooping and not letting him sleep and if he was still all by his lonesome. What help does he have at that palace of his? The flying monkeys? Maybe he gave her to someone who could take care of her better and told you she died?' Grizelda asked.

'If any of that happened, he would have just given Ellie back to me.' Mellie stuck her chin out.

'Except in the story that I know about the Wizard of Oz and the Emerald City, the girl who travelled to the Emerald City – her name was Ellie Smith, by the way – she came from outside of that dimension. Ellie used to live with her uncle and aunt in Texas, USA, Earth, before the hurricane lifted her whole house up and dropped it in the land where Oz lives,' Grizelda said.

'Ellie? Are you sure? In Baum's story the girl's name was Dorothy Gale, living with her uncle Henry and Aunt Em,' Grace said.

'That's not how Volkov tells the tale in the Russian version of the book,' Grizelda said and Mellie perked up. 'He might have based his tale on Baum's, but the names weren't all he changed.'

'There is a book about Oz? And there Ellie is adopted and alive somewhere?' Mellie asked, looking like Christmas came early.

'Two books.' Grace smirked.

'Two.' The hunger in Mellie's eyes was palpable.

Grizelda nodded when Grace lifted the tea pot. 'I didn't make the connection that your Ozzy was the Great Wizard of Oz,' the older woman said. 'Let's face it, he's not that great and he's as much of a wizard as you are a godmother - but I didn't realize who he was until you told all those lies about me and literally became the Wicked Witch of the West.'

'What's a Wicked Witch of the West?' Mellie asked. 'A ruling royal in Oz's kingdom?'

'Something like that.' Grace bit her lip so as not to laugh.

'How do I get there?' Mellie asked.

'What, the magic shoes didn't carry you over when you demanded they take you there?' Grace smirked.

Mellie pouted.

'You mean, you stole Ella's shoes and already tried to go to the Emerald City?' Grizelda asked.

'She was kind enough to let me borrow them,' Mellie mumbled.

'She only noticed they were gone after your brief visit to the palace following her engagement,' Grace interjected and Mellie went bright red.

Mellie crossed her arms. 'I didn't steal, I borrowed. I bet you don't know how I could get to Oz. I bet you don't know anything.'

'Don't answer that,' Grizelda told Grace and waved a finger at Mellie. 'You sly little minx, you don't think I know when you're trying to wheedle information out of us?'

'So, you don't know how to get there, do you?' Mellie asked.

'First, you need to tell us what do you plan to do about Oz. What are your intentions?' Grace asked. 'Find Oz, drag him here, live like one happy family? Or go there and punish him for abandoning you and not caring enough for Ellie?'

Grizelda assessed Mellie head to toe. 'If you have an ounce of good intent in you, you'll answer truthfully, girl.'

Mellie bit her lip. 'Well, I'm not angry at him anymore. It's only your speculation that he did something to Ellie or that he could have given her up.

When I figure it out how to go there, I'll go there, find him, find Ellie and we'll live happily ever after in his Emerald City.'

'Oz, Ellie and you, you mean?' Grizelda specified.

'Huh?'

'Just you and Ozzy and Ellie, right?' the old woman said, not unkindly. 'You don't intend to reunite the entire family. You'll leave Greta and Hans and Ella here? You'll leave them be?'

'Ella's married!' Mellie rolled her eyes.

'And Hans is in training and so is Greta. You dragging them anywhere would not be taken kindly,' Grizelda said. 'Besides, Greta wouldn't come with you for love or money. She knows.'

Mellie blanched. 'What do you mean Greta knows? Knows what?'

'Greta knows you are you,' Grace said. 'Ella thinks you sold your kids for food and knows you abandoned them to go after a man.'

'I didn't abandon them! I just followed their father. And I came back!'

'In disguise as their long-lost Aunt Mellie,' Grace pointed out.

Mellie *huffed*. 'That's why she was so distant with me when I went to congratulate her on her betrothal? She hates me now?' Mellie sat up straight and schooled her face to look impassive. 'The more reason for me to go. Don't you think?'

When she didn't get a quick enough 'yes', she flung herself onto the back of the chair and wailed, 'You are heartless, simply heartless!' Her whole body shook as she sobbed. 'Why don't you want me to go find my babyyyyyyyyy...'

'Well, 'coz you "placed" your other babies with "people who love them" rather than parent them yourself until they were good and ready to leave the nest, that's why. I definitely have difficulties believing that you have special feelings for a fourth child,' Grace said.

Mellie hiccoughed theatrically and continued shaking.

'But she would make a beautiful Wicked Witch of the West, don't you think?' Grizelda winked. 'Imagine the strife, the conflict, the epic fights, even more epic reconciliations...'

Mellie stilled.

'Considering her acting talents, she could double as Glinda, the Good Witch of the South.' Grace winked back.

'Oh, that would be Stella in my book,' Grizelda said.

'And if Mellie feigned naivete, she could even pass off for Theodora, the Good Witch of the North.'

'I don't know her by that name, I know her as Villina and the West one was Ginghema and the East one was Bastinda and according to my book they were all sisters...'

'Whom nobody ever saw together!' Grace and Grizelda said in unison.

'So, if Mellie could role play all four, nobody would be the wiser,' Grace said, thoughtfully. 'With her glamouring powers, she could, you know?'

'You'd better give me those books,' Mellie demanded.

'As in give you a manual?' Grizelda smirked. 'No problem. As long as you promise to give me the child when you and Oz get tired of playing family with a noisy and inquisitive toddler.'

When Grace cast Grizelda a long look, the older woman waved her away. 'I'll think of that when we come to it in four years.'

'What's in four years?' Mellie asked.

'Possibly nothing. Back to the books. Do you remember the language I taught you when you were little? The one you hated so much?' Grizelda asked.

'Why?'

'One of those books is in that language.'

Mellie growled. 'It will take me forever...'

'Not forever. Only until the other book gets delivered,' Grizelda said.

Mellie pouted.

'Well, I don't have both of them. The English version...'

'Baum's,' Grace supplied.

'Baum's version I would have to order from Earth via the Warriors. They're not a lending library, but they can deliver anything. If, IF we decide we're going to let you go.' Grizelda winked at Grace.

'You...you...you would deny me being reunited with the love of my life?' Mellie's mouth dropped and the waterworks started again.

'What do you think?' Grizelda asked Grace. 'Should we let her go wreak some havoc on Oz?'

'Why not?' Grace smiled. 'It's just a popular belief that villains shouldn't get their happily ever afters.'

'Villains? Villains?!?' Mellie sputtered. 'YOU were the wicked stepmother! I was the kind godmother! I'm not the villain!!!'

'You wouldn't be if you had just stayed their mother and not given any of them up to go manhunting,' Grizelda pointed out.

'I went after their father! So, we can be a family!'

'Except three of your kids don't want anything to do with you, just like you didn't want anything to do with me. Gods only know what has happened to your youngest,' Grizelda said.

'For me to find out, I need to find Oz. Tell me how to reach him!' Mellie demanded. 'How do I get there? What do I tell the shoes?'

'First, if you're going to jump dimensions, you would do well to tell the shoes that,' Grace said.

'Dimensions?'

Grizelda and Grace exchanged a look. 'She did say she was asleep for some of it. Maybe she slept through that?' Grizelda said. 'Oz is in another dimension. A different world. Which is also called Oz.'

'He has an entire dimension named after him?!?!' Mellie gaped. 'So, all I ever needed to tell the shoes was not "Take me to SEE Oz!" Or "Take me to OZZY", but "Take me to Oz"?!?!' Mellie looked disappointed.

Grace lifted an eyebrow. 'Is that what you said to the shoes before? You ordered them around?'

'Yes, and they didn't work! At all! And I couldn't go back to Ella to ask for more precise instructions!' Mellie pouted.

Grace smiled. 'That's because you stole them and forgot the magic word.'

'There's a magic word?' Mellie's jaw dropped.

'Of course, there is a magic word.' Her mother smiled and patted Mellie's head. 'The most common one any child knows.'

THE END

If you'd like to know if Mellie got her HEA or her comeuppance, continue with the Magic Mirrors Saga and the adventures of Ellie, Victor & Mellie in book #3: **Ash: Crooked Fates**

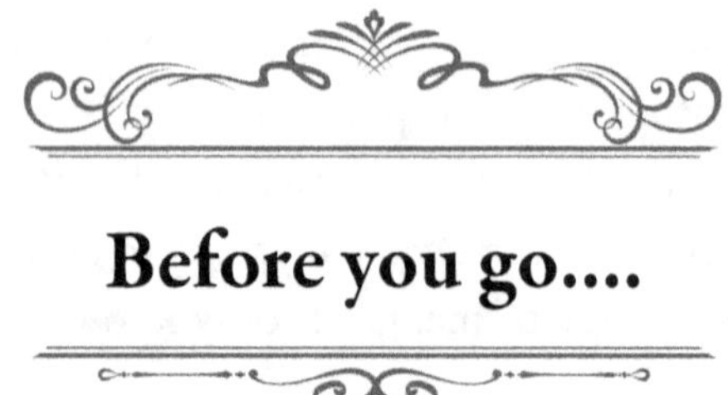

Before you go....

Thank you for choosing to read this book! Please leave a short review on Goodreads or Amazon or Bookbub or your blog or Instagram post or TikTok video (anywhere, really) as indie authors thrive on reviews — reader reviews help other readers find our books — not to mention that we absolutely wither and lose our will to live without them. Pretty please with sugar on top. 2-3 sentences of what you liked and how it made you feel should do it.

ACKNOWLEDGEMENTS

Thank you to all my readers for reading and loving my books and for telling me so over Insta and Facebook and in person!
A special thanks to Elli H. Radinger whose international bestseller The Wisdom of Wolves inspired me to rewrite some fairytale tropes of the big, bad menacing variety.
I would like to thank my beta readers, Astrid, Susan and Lynda - for pointing out where I could kill my darlings, the story is better because of it.
Thank you to my editor, Shreeya Nanda. Any and all mistakes that remain are entirely my own.
And last but not least - thank you to Rusham, for the amazing updated cover.

About the author

Sky is a USA Today bestselling indie author who writes retold fairytales and occasionally quirky romantasy where secrets are peeled back like onions. So far, Thumbelina has been updated for suspicious adults, a more sinister version of Cinderella, a multigenerational Red Riding Hood and a Wizard of Oz retelling have been published as full books and Snow Queen and Belle & Beast as novellas. A secret eco-warrior, she has co-published several charity anthologies that collect funds in support of our oceans, rainforests and communities plagued by wildfires. All her books are linked by some character or another and sometimes, in her standalones, she likes to make you choose, depending on your disposition (optimist vs pessimist) - 'coz the path that awaits depends on the decisions we take. (Well, except in the Magic Mirrors saga aka Cinders-Embers-Ash trilogy - because only Douglas Adams could pull off a trilogy in 5 parts.) She lives in Tallinn, Estonia, in a house with a small garden with her husband and two kids. No dog.

Besides fairytales, Sky keeps experimenting with different genres: myths & legends; steampunk; post-apocalyptic scifi; quirky fantasy romance and alternative history to name a few that are currently in the works.

You can connect with Sky and keep abreast of news in her multiverse on her author page: skysommers.com

www.ingramcontent.com/pod-product-compliance
Lightning Source LLC
Chambersburg PA
CBHW051834150726
47998CB00001B/411